MARIE-HÉLÈNE LEBEAULT

AUTHOR OF THE EVERS SERIES

CLARITY CASTLE

First published by Beaches and Trails Publishing 2021
Copyright © 2021 by Marie-Hélène Lebeault

Legal deposit - Bibliothèque et Archives nationales du Québec, 2021
Legal deposit - Bibliothèque et Archives Canada, 2021
First Edition
Paperback ISBN 978-1-990656-37-8

Proofreading by Sophie Snow
Cover art by MiblArt

BEACHES AND TRAILS
PUBLISHING

ABOUT THE AUTHOR

Positive, uplifting books and stories.

Marie-Helene Lebeault lives in Quebec, Canada and is the mother of two young adults. A retired teacher, she now spends her days writing, translating academic manuals, and lending her voice to corporate training videos. She enjoys reading, hiking, and going to the beach. She is also an avid rollercoaster fiend and is on a mission to visit all the Six Flags amusement parks with her daughter. Every year, she travels for three weeks on a solo adventure to a new part of the world.

Follow on Social Media, she'd love to hear from you!

Website Email Newsletter

ALSO BY THE AUTHOR

The Evers Series

The Ancestors' Key

The Academy

The Time Walker

The World Jumper

The Blood Magick Trilogy

The Blood Mage

Blood Magick

Blood Legacy

Standalones

Clarity Castle

Anthologies

What Happens Next?: Readers Decide Which Story Becomes A Book

Novellas

Stranded with a Shifter: A YA Holiday Romance

Picture Books

Fairy Grandmother: Millie Goes to Antarctica

Fairy Grandmother: Millie Goes to the North Pole

Fairy Grandmother: Millie Goes to China

(Available in English, French, Spanish, German, and Italian)

"Time and space are illusions. Everything exists at the same time. We only see what we are tuned to the vibration of to see.
As we change our ideas, we change our vibrations, we start to see a different world, literally. Because we have shifted our consciousness, our focus, to a different version of Earth that exists simultaneously with the version we were on a moment ago.
And we are experiencing a progression through different versions of Earth."

Bashar, channelled by Daryl Anka

FOREWORD

Dearest Reader,

As some of you may know, I'm a Canadian author. Most of my books are written in American English for accessibility. However, as Clarity Castle is set in the Eastern Townships of Quebec where I live, I thought it was fitting to write it in Canadian English. If you hail from the UK or Australia, you won't find anything amiss. My American readers may raise an eyebrow here and there at the peculiar way we Canadians write a few words.

Hopefully, you won't find it too distressing.

I value your readership and hope you enjoy Claire's multiple timelines!

Marie-Hélène

CHAPTER ONE

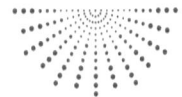

I'D LIKE TO SAY I NOTICED IT RIGHT AWAY, THAT I SOMEHOW FELT THE strangeness in the air. However, the truth was that I had just gotten a less than desirable grade in my latest math test, and I was walking it off. The one-kilometre walk to the woods had taken the edge off my disappointment, and I was able to bring the self-recriminations to a low simmer. As I entered the woods, the world disappeared. There was nothing magical about that; it was just nature. It instantly grounded me, the earth pulling out my worries like so much fertilizer.

I loved walking these woods. There used to be more of them, but our town had been developing like crazy the last few years. As it stood, the little patch of heaven spread out over roughly eighty-four thousand square meters.

Most of the time, I would walk around the woods, looping the various trails for about thirty minutes, and then I'd go home. But when I had more time or needed a longer break, I'd cut through the quarry and follow the trail that led to the lake.

That's where I was heading on that fateful day. There's a barbed-wire fence around the perimeter of the quarry, so the aspiring trespasser would have to know where to cross. Over the years, people started leaving clues. Just off the trail, there was a red ribbon tied to a tree. When the trail got muddy, good Samaritans placed rocks or fallen logs to ease the way.

It was always a little blinding when I came out of the woods and into the clearing. Once my eyes adjusted to the light, I saw the lake across the field of flowers. Wait, that's not right. There should be a clearing full of weeds, a road, and a parking lot between me and the lake. I blinked, thinking I'd lulled myself into my own imaginings. But there it was again—an expanse of perfectly manicured lawns and patches of flowers and shrubbery.

Compelled to investigate, I took a few steps and felt an unfamiliar firmness under my feet. There was a stone path etched in the dewy grass. Looking up as I walked the path, I turned away from the lake towards what should have been the quarry and stopped dead in my tracks. To my utter astonishment, instead of a pit of rocks, I saw a castle. Perhaps it was merely a mansion; I honestly didn't know the difference. It was enormous.

Poor math grade notwithstanding, I was pretty good at math. I remembered reading that the quarry site was twenty-five acres. The owner wanted to build cooperative housing on it a few years back, but nothing came of it. My house sat on a two-acre lot. This house, or whatever the structure was called, had to be at least five times as big as our lot.

It looked like it was about four stories high. The huge stone structure was either square or rectangle in shape; it was hard to tell from where I stood. I started walking towards it. Each corner had a circular turret. *The view of the lake must be amazing from there,* I thought. On either side of the carriage doors were a pair of stone staircases that seemed to lead to a walled-in patio.

I followed the stone path to a larger path of pebbles or crushed stone. This one looked like a road or a driveway. One way led up to the castle, one way led to the lake, and another led to a group of smaller buildings to the left of the castle. I was torn. Where should I investigate first?

It occurred to me then that I was either dreaming or had somehow been transported to the past. I really should have taken the time to

2

learn about our town's history when we moved here ten years ago. In my defence, I was six years old at the time, and this was never covered in school.

If I were dreaming, it wouldn't matter where I went. I could explore at my leisure, and nothing could go wrong. If I had been whisked to the past, I was likely trespassing, and that could turn out badly. I had read enough time-travelling and historical romance novels to know I would need to blend in, and quickly.

I looked down at myself and saw I was still wearing my jeans, t-shirt, and sneakers. If this was a dream, I could close my eyes and choose a more suitable attire. But which one? What time was this? In any case, there was no time in the distant past where tight-fitting trousers and a V-neck top were appropriate. At the very least, I should choose a loose-fitting dress that covered most of my exposed skin.

I closed my eyes and tried to imagine a simple gown that would make me look respectable in any century. I envisioned a blue Victorian dress over a muslin chemise and petticoats. I twirled on myself to let the skirts fan out, but I saw no change in my attire as I opened my eyes. *Shit. Not a dream.*

Should I go back to the woods? Perhaps I had inadvertently walked through a portal or crossed a veil. I retraced my steps but felt no different as I entered the woods again. Observing attentively, I saw no difference. The best way to find out would be to head home.

After about ten minutes, uneasiness crept upon me. I should have reached the beginning of the new street by now, but I was still in the woods. I kept walking. The path, or rather a well-worn strip of forest floor, continued ahead. I followed it to the road. It was hard to find my bearings, but I was sure this should be highway 104 heading to Knowlton and Sutton. Instead, it was a wide dirt road, with no cars in sight. There was nothing but woods on either side of the road, in both directions. This was a Cowansville of the past. One where my home didn't exist.

When one was lost, one should head to the nearest store to ask for directions. Barring that, the nearest home. That was the castle. Surely this road led to the castle, as it was the only one I had encountered thus far. I started walking.

After about twenty minutes, I reached a lane. Squinting, I could see the castle at the end of it and headed down the lane. I would at least be arriving at the front door. As it grew nearer, I was again struck by its size. Seen from the front, it was majestic. The lane went around a circular topiary garden, though a narrow path went through it.

Once inside the garden, I realized it was much larger than I had estimated. My head barely cleared the manicured shrubs bordering the garden. It was reassuring. I didn't feel quite as exposed as I had while I had been approaching the castle, though my presence had yet to be detected as far as I could see.

I hovered at the edge of the garden. Once I crossed the lane, I'd have to go up the stairs and knock on the door. I had a feeling there wouldn't be a doorbell.

I felt the hairs on the back of my neck rise. It was that creepy feeling you got when someone was watching you. Instinctively, I looked up and saw movement in one of the upstairs windows. Like a ghost, the person vanished behind a swish of drapes.

Someone was home. Chin up, I made my way to the door and grasped the ancient brass door knocker. I raised it, then knocked hard three times. Straining to hear, I could detect no sound coming from inside. Clasping my hands behind my back so they wouldn't shake, I checked my posture and plastered a polite smile on my face.

The butler swung the door open, gave me a once over, and bowed as he moved out of the way to let me enter.

"Good morning," I said nervously.

The man, oblivious to my greeting, extended his arm and motioned for me to precede him in the hall. Once he had closed the door, he pointed to a large upholstered bench. I sat. He bowed and left.

Though the outside of the castle looked downright medieval, the inside had more polish. Where I had expected wall-to-wall stone, I found the hall to be entirely decked in a dark, well-polished wood. I was itching to get up and look around, but I stayed put. I was trespassing and poorly attired; it wouldn't do to be caught snooping as well.

From where I sat, my eyes followed one of the staircases to the second-floor landing. There were portraits up there, but I couldn't see the faces clearly. I saw a bit of a blue skirt peeking out from behind one of the columns. I was about to call out to my little ghost when I heard someone approaching on my right.

"You're right on time," said the elegant lady as she glided across the floor, arms outstretched as though to embrace me.

On impulse, I stood as she neared me. I opened my mouth, but all that came out was, "I... I.."

"Goodness, what *are* you wearing, Clare?" she asked.

"How do you know my name?" I asked, finally finding my voice.

Her smile dimmed a little, and she peered at me, pursing her lips. "I see," she replied. Turning on her heels, she walked back the way she had come and called out, "come along, Clare."

How does *she know my name?* I wondered. She clearly thought she knew me. Perhaps we had met, but I had forgotten. I checked my head for a bump and found none. This really was most peculiar.

The lady had stridden to the far end of the hall before she noticed I had not followed. "Don't just stand there; come meet the others," she beckoned.

CHAPTER TWO

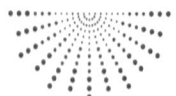

THE LADY LED THE WAY TO A BRIGHT YELLOW SITTING ROOM. THERE were a dozen or so girls in the room already. A few were reading; some were playing cards.

One was playing the piano, one the violin, while another was singing. I didn't know the song, but they were good. One girl was painting a landscape by the window, and another was furiously scribbling in a notebook. A restless one was pacing back and forth, checking the time on her sports watch. Amid the chaos, one girl was meditating, and the last girl was doing needlepoint and humming happily along with the song.

Though they all seemed to be about my age, no two girls were wearing the same dress style. Looking at each of them in turn, I wondered if I'd stumbled onto a TV set. It looked like they were about to shoot a girl power commercial or something.

Each girl seemed to represent a stereotypical activity with its corresponding attire. I had no idea what my jeans and t-shirt look was saying about me. That was probably why the lady had asked about it. Was I auditioning for a part I didn't know about? The restless girl was wearing a futuristic catsuit straight out of a sci-fi movie.

"Everyone, this is Clare," said the lady, putting a hand on my shoulder. "She's a—" she paused and looked at me, trying to assess my provenance.

"Student?" I supplied, biting my lip.

"No dear, what's your skill?" she replied.

My skill? I thought in anguish. I had no skills. That was the problem. I was an average girl, living an average life. Hence the generic outfit.

Having stopped what they were doing to listen to the lady, the girls started moving closer and calling out their skills as though it wasn't already obvious. The restless girl said she was a gymnast. These girls had their stuff together. I had no idea where I was going.

Before I could stop myself, I blurted, "worrying." I immediately clasped a hand over my mouth.

I was about to ask for their names. Surely, I wouldn't be addressing them by skill. Then, Singer approached me, hand outstretched.

"So pleased to meet you!" she said. As I shook her hand and looked up to her, now up close, the automatic greeting, I was about to provide died on my lips.

I stared at her in confusion. She was me. I was she. I stared dumbly at our identical hands clasped together, then back at the lady who had brought me here. Dear God, she was *me*, too! An older me. I let go of Singer's hand and looked around wildly at each of the girls' faces. They were *all* me! Most were wearing looks of understanding. The writer observed, ready to pounce on my reaction to jot it down for posterity in her notebook. The card-playing Clares giggled.

"Clare, perhaps you should sit down," said older me, leading me to the sofa. Needlepoint offered a cup of tea which I took but did not immediately drink. The piano girl came over with a glass of an amber liquid which had to be alcohol. I frowned at her and shook my head. She shrugged and knocked it back as she strode to the piano and started playing. Violin joined her, and most of the others went back to their previous occupations.

I was left with the older me and Singer. Needlepoint sat down and resumed her quiet humming.

"Rest assured, we all had the same reaction," Singer said kindly.

As the words left my lips, I knew that this was the lamest of questions, but I just didn't know what else to say. "Am I dreaming?" I asked, taking a sip of tea to occupy my hands that were starting to shake.

Older me—she really was quite beautiful, as vain as that sounds—was the first to respond.

"Yes, and no," she said cryptically. She stood then. She put her hands together and took a breath. I recognized the pose immediately; a lecture.

My mom did that all the time. She called them 'teaching moments.' In the middle of a regular conversation, or even a movie, she'd stop and turn into lecturing mom. Not the kind of lecture where she scolded me, but the kind one would find in a university class. She'd share some bit of knowledge or experience that was meant to change my life in a profound way.

I loved my mom; she was truly an amazing woman. But when she went into lecture mode, I cringed. Not because her lectures were irrelevant or uninteresting, they were often fascinating and entertaining. But because they seemed to come from a place that assumed I needed the information. Bless her heart, like most parents, she failed to realize that times had changed, and they were evolving fast. Her wisdom, though sound, would likely never be put to use.

I placed the teacup on the coffee table and assumed the avid listener position. Earnest facial expression, back straight, hands clasped in my lap.

"This," she started, hands out on either side to encompass the room, "is Clarity Castle. It is situated out of time and space. For you, it appears to be near your home, but likely in an unusual spot."

I nodded. "In my reality, there is an old quarry where the castle stands. And that whole space by the lake is a community nature park," I supplied.

"Right. The Castle is the same for all of us, but its location may differ for some of us. You could say it's our home base or headquarters," she said.

"Headquarters for what?" I asked. Was I part of some secret order of clones?

"I don't know if you know this, but the name Clare is derived from the Latin word *clarus*, which means bright, clear, or famous. That is why the castle is named Clarity. Every one of us is seeking clarity in some way or another. And this is where we find it."

She let that sink in for a moment. *Do I seek clarity?* I wondered to myself. After a moment of reflection, I had to admit she spoke the truth. I hated it when people didn't communicate clearly. I preferred to deal with someone who was straight-up rude than with half-truths and double-entendres. I must have been nodding because older me continued.

"The Castle is our true home. It is where we begin. Where we come back to rest, heal, grow, learn, and explore. As we go out in the world, we often forget about it and only return when we are asleep, through what appear to be dreams. Eventually, we become aware of it and can return anytime. That is what we call the Awakening."

I frowned, aware now that this wasn't clear and that it was annoying. And I was annoyed at being annoyed. I sighed and shook it off.

"Well, then. Am I awake or asleep?" I asked, hoping for a more comprehensive answer.

"You are awake, but you haven't yet, Awoken. You are currently walking in the woods near your house, in a state of relaxed contemplation that doesn't require all of you to be present. A part of you has come here," she replied.

"Are you saying I'm walking around like a zombie while my mind is here?" I asked, horrified that I could have left my body unattended. What if I crossed the road and got hit by a car?

Singer scooted closer on the sofa and placed a reassuring hand on my arm. "No, Clare. It's not your mind that has left your body. It's your consciousness," she said soothingly.

My consciousness? Dude, seriously? How can I walk around without my consciousness? "Are you saying I'm having an out-of-body experience in broad daylight?" I asked, my tone rising a little.

Older me squared her shoulders and smiled. "Not exactly. I will not be able to explain everything to your satisfaction today. That is why you are here to learn, or I should say, *remember*. Let's begin with the concept of a soul. How would you define that?" she asked.

"I guess it's that intangible part of us. When we die, it follows us to our next body," I said tentatively. I wasn't the most spiritual person. Ironically, this had been a regular topic of my mom's lectures. Thanks for the info, Mom.

"That is a good place to start. I want to add a few elements to your understanding, though. With every new body comes a new life, personality, and goals. In your definition, when a new life begins, the other one ends. In truth, no life ever ends.

"For every new incarnation, a new consciousness is born. Consciousness is a new expression of the same soul. If the soul was a cookie, each consciousness would be a different flavour of the cookie. But that's still a cookie, do you understand?" she asked. I nodded.

"Just because you ate a cookie doesn't mean it no longer exists. On the one hand, the matter that made up the cookie is now in your stomach being digested. It has been transformed. On the other hand, the memory of the cookie is intact. The past cookie is real. And finally, before you saw the cookie and ate it, you knew it existed. That future cookie is also real," she continued.

"You're talking about the time continuum, how all things exist at once. Past, present, and future," I said.

"Yes!" exclaimed Singer.

"That's why a new consciousness has to be created with every new incarnation, because the old one is still in use," I ventured, getting excited now.

"Correct," said older me. "And the soul is always aware of each incarnation because they are part of it."

"Wait, are you saying that the Castle is our soul?" I asked, standing up abruptly. I had it now!

"No, the Castle is our consciousness," stated Singer, barely above a whisper.

I sat back down. "But who are all these people, then?" I asked, waving at the room in general.

"We are all probable versions of the same consciousness," said older me.

My eyes closed, and a headache lodged itself between my eyes. "Probable versions?" I asked.

"Parallel versions would be more accurate. Are you familiar with the many-worlds interpretation of Quantum Mechanics?" asked older me.

My head whipped around as realization dawned on me. Every single thing my mom had been blathering on about was true. When she had me watch 'What the Bleep Do We Know,' I had taken it for just another sci-fi movie. It was old, and the visual effects were lacking. But the message had been clear: there are unlimited versions of everyone.

"You're talking about the multiverse. Are you saying everyone in this room is a spin-off of the same person? Including me?" I asked.

"Yes, we are," put in Needlepoint, who I had entirely forgotten was sitting in a wing chair a few feet away. In fact, I had entirely tuned out the lot of mes around the room. Their collective sounds now seemed deafening as I turned back to look at other versions of me.

Of course, that's what they were. They couldn't be cloned, and clones would have been identical. Each me was a little different. Sure, the basic structure was there: blond hair, green eyes, about five feet six inches, same face. But the hair varied in length, shade, and style. No two had the same shape. Some were lean, and some were plump. Some were clearly muscular. The posture was also different from one to the next.

"Doesn't the concept of a multiverse imply unlimited versions of a person? I see a dozen or so. And you, of course," I said to older me. "What should I call you?" I asked belatedly.

"You may call me Teacher. You are correct. However, we believe it would be overwhelming to meet all of them at once. Besides, we can't all be here at the same time. No, the people in the room are a selection of Clares, aged fifteen, living in this neighbourhood."

"Where are the others?" I asked, curious.

"For simplicity's sake, we've devoted a room to each same-aged

11

group of Clares who are in the process of Awakening. For example, in the green sitting room, you'll find the twelve-year-olds. Twenty-somethings are on the second floor, the thirties on the third and the forties on the fourth," she explained.

"What about older Clares?" I asked.

"No one has ever awakened beyond their fiftieth birthday. Elder Clares are usually Teachers, Guides, or Managers. Though, I must add that there is no age limit for Teachers and Guides. You could be a five-year-old Guide or a twenty-year-old Teacher," she replied.

"How old are you? Where is your room?" I asked in fascination.

"I'm thirty-eight. Our room is pink," she replied.

I filed this away for future reference. "If I haven't yet awakened, how did I get here while I am still awake?" I asked.

"That is unusual. The truth is we couldn't wait any longer. We need your help," she said.

CHAPTER THREE

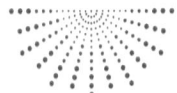

I WAS SITTING ON ONE OF THE BENCHES IN FRONT OF THE LAKE STARING at the loons. The sun at my back was warm and I must have dozed off. Checking my watch, I saw it was almost five. I hadn't meant to be gone this long. I texted mom so she wouldn't be worried if she got home from work before me.

Mom was an HR hiring consultant. She helped companies hire the best candidates. She had a knack for finding diamonds among the coal. She also took on private clients with unusual skillsets and set them where they would shine best.

She mostly worked from home, except when employers wanted her to sit in on interviews. Today, I think she was interviewing for an engineer at the big dairy plant.

She was tossing a salad when I came in. "Hi, honey," she called from the kitchen.

I took off my shoes and padded into the kitchen, then gave her a big hug.

"That was a long walk. Did something happen at school?" she asked, dividing the leftover meatloaf between two plates. When she was done, I put the first one in the microwave.

"I got a seventy-two in my math test," I said, getting utensils from the drawer to set the table.

"I know you were hoping for better, but it's not a bad grade," she replied.

The microwave beeped and I swapped the plates. Mom loaded salad onto the plate, and I placed it on the table.

"Mom, you know I need a seventy-five average to get into the advanced math and science classes next year," I said, slapping my thighs with my hands.

She gave me her glass to fill and I retrieved the second plate on my way back. She heaved a mountain of salad on it and we went to sit at the table.

"The keyword here is average. You got eighty-one and eighty-three in the first two report cards. You'll do fine in the third one. It's only one exam, stop worrying!" she soothed.

Easier said than done. Since I had no idea what I wanted to do with my life, I had to keep all my options open. The best way to do this was to take all the advanced classes next year to get into any program I wanted when I got to college. Hopefully, by then, I'd have a clearer picture of the future.

All my friends had already chosen their career paths. Mel was going to be an actress, Julie a dentist, and Sam was heading for law school. I had high hopes for the assessments we had taken with the guidance counsellor, but the results barely narrowed my choices. I would basically succeed at anything I did.

Which, of course, was what Mom has been telling me most of my life. I'm pretty sure that's what all parents told their children. It also said I would do best working with people, like I needed a three-hour test to tell me that! I wasn't into computers, and though I enjoyed my time alone, I was a social creature through and through. I liked helping people. A great quality, though not a career choice.

I asked Mom about her day to change the subject and she asked if I had a lot of homework. When I didn't, we'd watch movies together in the evening. Tonight, I needed to prep for an upcoming physics test.

We did the dishes and I headed for my room to study. Mom took her glass of wine with her as she went to the back deck and settled in to read a book. Mom loved to read. She could sit in the same spot for three hours, moving only to turn the pages or take a sip of whatever she was drinking. Coffee, tea, or wine, depending on the time of day. Never water, though that's all she drank the rest of the day. It was like she saved the best for her reading time. Like a date. I wish she'd go on actual dates.

We'd swipe through pictures on her dating app. Though we had a great time gently disparaging the candidates, she never found any that she liked. She said she knew too much about human nature to fall for clever dating profiles. And appearances could be deceiving.

"Besides," she'd once told me, hugging her favourite book to her chest, "I'm waiting for my own Jamie Fraser." I had rolled my eyes. I didn't know much about Jamie Fraser, but I knew he made a lot of women, and many men, swoon. I actually couldn't blame her reasoning. I had yet to find a boy I liked at school. Perhaps Mom's pickiness was rubbing off on me. It was convenient, as I'd need to focus on school for the foreseeable future and had no time for boys.

Mom came in to say good night around nine o'clock. We each had our own bedtime routines. Mine was a shower and scrolling through the social media posts I had missed while at school or studying. I was usually out by ten o'clock. I could get engrossed with something and stay up until eleven, but that would throw the next day's schedule completely out of whack and I resisted temptation as much as possible.

Tonight was easy. I was super tired and fell asleep as soon as my head hit the pillow, still clutching my phone.

* * *

I WAS AT THE CLEARING, BUT I COULDN'T REMEMBER HOW I GOT THERE. When I saw the Castle, the day's events came back to me. *Why didn't I remember before now?* I wondered. Probably because I hadn't yet Awoken, if Teacher was to be believed.

I checked my outfit and saw it was the same I had worn earlier that day. I debated trying to change it and gave up the notion. They'd seen me wearing this and that's how they would know it was me, the Worrier.

As I walked toward the back of the Castle, I remembered what Teacher had said just before I woke up by the lake, that they needed my help. I had no idea how I could be useful to a bunch of over-achieving alternate versions of me. Maybe one of them needed a babysitter. *Wait, do any of my other selves have siblings? A boyfriend? A dad?* I wondered. That last one had sneaked in, thinking I wouldn't notice. I scolded my subconscious and focused on finding a door knocker on the back doors.

I stood in front of the giant-sized opening. The massive oak doors were reinforced with intricate iron patterns and had no discernable handle. On impulse, I placed both hands on one of the doors and pushed. I was rewarded with a little movement. I turned and pushed the door with my butt until the opening was large enough for me to slip through.

From the outside, I had heard no sign of life within. But once inside, I was assaulted by the chaos of what seemed like a hundred children, all girls, playing in the courtyard. Someone yelled "close the door," and I quickly pushed it back the same way I had opened it.

I leaned against the door and stared open-mouthed at my selves. The courtyard was at least the size of a football field. The doors I had just entered through were likely the carriage doors I had seen earlier, as pebbled roads framed the perimeter of the space. Older children were walking or cycling along the path. Some were older, perhaps Teachers or Guides, and pushing strollers. A few groups were playing jump rope and other such games.

The middle part was divided into four sections. The two closest to me were gardens with large grassed areas where children were play-ing. Tall trees provided shade and some of them featured swings. There were benches all around the area where we could sit and read, or watch the other children playing.

The two sections closest to the main area of the Castle had more modern playground features such as swings, jungle gyms, and sandboxes. They should have looked out of place in a castle courtyard, but they were medieval in theme and blended well with the rest of the space.

There were doors that led to the wings on either side of the courtyard, but I made my way to the one in the main section. Curious to see myself at various ages, I followed the path through the gardens and playground.

You would think that seeing so many replicas of yourself would get boring or make you feel ordinary after a while. But each face I saw was fascinating. They were me, but not me. It occurred to me then that they were not completely identical. Unlike the girls I had met the last time I was here, the children did not all have blond hair, nor were they all Caucasian. Thankfully, despite their differences in personality and demeanour, they seemed to play well together.

I had always longed for a sister I could play with when I was younger, one I could confide in now that I was older. These children were so fortunate to have all these perfectly suited playmates!

I had reached the path and turned for one last look at my selves and smiled. They were so beautiful, and I felt so much love for each and every one of them that I felt my eyes tear up. I reminded myself that a dozen or so 'sisters' awaited me in the yellow room. Joy invaded my chest and I felt the sudden urge to run up the stairs and launch myself into the Castle. This was going to be fun.

CHAPTER FOUR

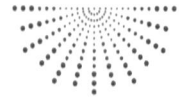

I WOKE UP FEELING MORE CHEERFUL THAN I HAD ANY RIGHT TO BE. I had French and Phys. Ed today, my least favorite subjects. Both required a lot of teamwork participation, which would have been fine if any of my friends were in my class. I was the only in my group to have elected for French as a First Language, a decision I regretted on the very first day.

Since we lived in a French-speaking province, it had seemed prudent to be as fluent as possible to increase not only my career options but the number of colleges I could get into. However, it soon became apparent that my classmates were all already bilingual and had mastered the content with very little effort. I, on the other hand, sucked at French.

Like everyone else, I had taken the mandatory French as a Second Language class since grade one. I'd also performed reasonably well, which was why my selection had been approved. Nonetheless, I was ill-prepared for the rigors of FFL which required reading literary novels, both French and Québécois, as well as writing essays, and debating with the same level of skill as we would in English Language Arts. My limited oral proficiency made me a liability to any team project and, instead of providing me with models to emulate, simply exacerbated my performance anxiety.

The horrors of Phys. Ed were the product of yet another ill-advised decision. Each semester, we could choose from three activities. Julie had chosen tennis because she and her family belonged to a club and she figured it would be an easy A. Mel had chosen track and field as she's a natural-born athlete. Sam was in the sports study program and spends most afternoons at the pool. I had chosen yoga because it seemed like a relaxing, individual activity where performance would be less important than mindfulness. That's what the brochure said, anyway.

It turned out that some yoga enthusiasts were focused entirely on appearances—it's all about the outfit—and perfect form. I mastered neither the outfits nor the form and always left the class feeling terribly inadequate.

Complaining to Mom about it was never a good idea. As soon as I expressed any displeasure with the high school experience, she'd go into Warrior Mom mode and insist on talking or, god-forbid, *writing a pointed email* to someone. Anyone. To whoever dared to make her perfect child feel less than loved, empowered, and valued.

The first few times she did it, I felt vindicated, at first. Then I started worrying that the teachers might be mean to me because of it. It never happened, but I begged her to stop it.

She promised to put away her lethal pen and just listen when I needed to talk. Which she was incapable of doing. She had to provide advice or a five-step action plan to fix the situation. Sometimes her suggestions were helpful, other times not so much.

This must make her sound as though her life revolved around me. It didn't. Though she didn't go out much and hadn't dated in years, Mom enjoyed her own company. A lot. She was always taking off on some solo adventure somewhere or trying new things. She had a fearlessness that I envied. She was so passionate about everything, including me.

So even if I didn't always feel loved, empowered, and valued at school, I knew I was the apple of my mother's eye.

I scrolled through the social media posts of the previous evening. My friends did not adhere to a strict ten o'clock bedtime. Sam was proposing we had lunch outside today and suggesting, nay insisting, we packed a lunch and met in our usual spot on the back lawn.

This was great news indeed. Not only would it make the day more bearable, but it had been a while since we all had a free lunch hour together. Sam was often away on competitions, Mel had drama practice, and I tutored younger students in English Language Arts. When none of us was available, Julie ate by herself then headed to the library. She read almost as much as my mom.

When I came out of my room, Mom was waiting with the usual hug. I headed to the bathroom and joined her in the kitchen. Because she was up since the crack of dawn, Mom could get a little chatty when she saw me emerge from my room.

I had to sit her down once and gently let her know that when I woke up, I didn't have the benefit of two productive hours and three cups of coffee under my belt. All I had were fond memories of a warm bed and vague apprehensions on the day ahead.

She had understood. Now we spent the first thirty minutes in silence. After I ate, I asked if we had anything I could pack for a cold lunch. Mom was a good cook, but she didn't like doing dishes so she made huge batches of food when the mood struck. Packing a lunch was usually a breeze. I simply reached for any of the dozens of glassware containers, as well as smaller containers she filled with nuts, homemade cookies, or treats, and filled my water bottle. Done.

Packing a cold lunch would prove a little more challenging. Or so I thought. In minutes, mom had assembled a bento-box-like feast that would do any dietician proud. I was reminded of the amazing lunches she used to pack for me at school. Tasty, nutritious, and fun. I thanked her profusely for feeding me so well. I did this regularly because I had seen what other kids at school ate and they were clearly left to their own devices.

While I was getting dressed, she asked if I wanted a ride to school. She was heading into town for more interviews. I told her I'd take the bus. Contrary to most high school kids, I liked taking the bus. It was only a fifteen-minute ride, and I got to pop in my headphones and take a power nap. When I finally got to school, I was ready to take on the world. Or French.

TODAY, MONSIEUR MARCEL HAD US READING *BARBE BLEUE*, A FRENCH folk tale written by Charles Perreault. It was the story of Bluebeard, a wealthy man who, soon after his marriage, went away, leaving his wife the keys to all the doors in his castle yet forbid her to open any of them. She took no heed and found the bodies of his former wives. Upon his return, Bluebeard noticed a bloody smudge on one of the keys and threatened to cut off her head for her disobedience. Just as Bluebeard was about to strike the final blow, the wife was saved by the timely arrival of her brothers.

It's not a bad story, except that we had to read aloud in turn, something I hated. Then we discussed the moral of the story before splitting up into teams to order the twelve strips of paper he had placed in an envelope to reconstruct the story. Then, in pairs, we had to make lists of the physical and emotional attributes of each of the characters. For homework, we had to write a three-hundred-word response to the following prompt: compare and contrast the couple dynamics with those of today.

After a quick chat at the break with Mel at my locker, I headed to Phys. Ed. At least here I could give my poor brain a rest. Not only did my mind get a rest, but my body did too. Today's class was about restorative poses. *Easy-peasy.* The class ended with a guided relaxation in corpse pose, my favorite. Now, if only Ms. Maxwell could stop talking, it would be bliss. My wish was granted when there was a knock at the door. Called away, the teacher instructed us to let our minds drift into silent meditation. I promptly fell asleep.

CHAPTER FIVE

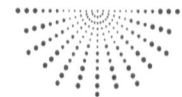

I WAS LYING ON THE GRASS, BASKING IN THE SUNSHINE. THE WARMTH felt divine on my face and arms and all I could hear was the two-note song of a faraway mockingbird. *Wait, birdsong?*

I got up abruptly. I was in the grassy fields behind the Castle. *I must have fallen asleep in yoga class.* Funny how I forgot all about the Castle when I was awake, but when I was asleep I could recall everything.

Conscious I would likely not have a lot of time, I hurried towards the Castle. The courtyard was empty. I sprinted down the road and entered the first door on my right. Once my eyes adjusted to the dark interior, I set off in the direction I thought led to the front of the house. There was an endless number of doors on either side of me as I walked briskly down the wide hallway. I resisted the temptation to open the doors. I knew what I'd find.

What I needed now was a Teacher, a Guide, or even a Manager. I had to find out how to come here voluntarily, or at least learn to stay longer at night. I saw a foyer up ahead, though I didn't think it was the main hall. When I reached it, I saw it was a landing. On one side there were stairs with the most beautiful stained-glass window I had ever seen. It depicted a girl and horse galloping in a field very much like the one behind the castle. The girl, me of course, had a look of utter joy and something akin to freedom as she rode with her hair blowing in the wind, crouched low on her steed.

I was so mesmerized by the window that I forgot why I had come and jumped at the sound of the elevator's ding. Wait, elevator?

* * *

I WAS WOKEN UP BY THE SOUND OF THE TRIANGLE THE TEACHER clanged to wake the students at the end of class. I was not the only one who fell asleep, teenagers were notorious for not getting enough sleep. Except me. I got enough sleep but here I was falling asleep everywhere like I suffered from narcolepsy. Perhaps I should make an appointment with the school nurse. I made a mental note of it as I changed and rushed back to my locker to grab my lunch.

When I got to the table, my friends were already there. They were talking about the new Avatar sequel coming out.

"I can't wait to see that!" I said, opening my lunch container. The conversation immediately stopped as they all stared it.

"On the one hand, I want to tease you and ask if you stole a kindergartener's lunch. On the other hand, I want to beg you to swap with me like we did in grade school," joked Sam.

His lunch was a store-bought egg-salad sandwich, a lime-colored Jell-O, and a bag of salt-and-vinegar chips. I had half a mind to agree to a swap if he was serious. That looked sinfully delicious. I bit my lip and thought better of it. I had a theory that Mom's nutritious food was what had kept acne at bay until now. The theory was only reinforced by glancing at Sam's pimpled face.

I embraced my lunch and hissed out, "my precious," which cracked everybody up and we moved on to other topics of discussion.

The rest of the day was greatly improved. Mel, Julie, and I had two periods of English today. Our class had just finished reading *The Giver*, one of my favorite books. The afternoon was dedicated to watching the movie adaptation and comparing it to the book.

When I got home, I was too restless to start on homework, so I headed back out. Intent on my usual thirty-minute walk, I opted for a brisk neighborhood walk. When possible, I liked to help Mom with dinner.

The walk felt good after sitting all afternoon and when I got home, I felt refreshed and focused. Mom's weekly menu, posted on the fridge, indicated that we were having lasagna tonight. Yum! I pre-heated the oven, transferred the baking dish from the fridge to the oven, and set a timer for thirty minutes. That would give me just enough time to write my response for the French class.

Mom got home right when the oven timer was beeping. She took out the lasagna and started tossing a salad. I told her I was not quite finished with my French assignment and I conveniently finished just when she told me dinner is ready.

Over dinner, I told mom about lunch with my friends and the rest of my day. Her day was uneventful. She's glad the interviews were over. She planned on working that evening. If she sent her recom-mendations tonight, she'd be done with this client and could take it easy tomorrow. That meant one of two things, either she'd head for a day at a local spa, or she'd bake all day.

Once the dishes were done, we went our separate ways until it was time to say goodnight. We were very much creatures of habit.

CHAPTER SIX

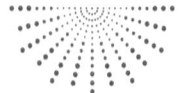

THIS TIME, I WAS BACK ON THE LANE LEADING TO THE FRONT DOOR. There had to be a faster way to get where I was going. When I reached the Castle, I didn't bother knocking. The door was unlocked and I made my way to the yellow sitting room.

There were about a dozen or so girls there again, but some were new. One was dressed as a ballet dancer. I couldn't believe there was a world where I was that lean and graceful. Another was wearing a lab coat with a pair of protective glasses pushed up in her hair. I made a mental note to ask her for help on my upcoming Physics exam.

My eyes rested on an emo girl sitting cross-legged on the floor, back to the wall. She was wearing skinny black jeans, black Converse shoes, and a t-shirt that read "Black is My Happy Color." The bangs of obviously dyed black hair obscured part of her face, but it was still me. With bangs! And a nose piercing. And heavy black eye makeup. Unbelievable.

I shook it off and looked for Singer. She seemed to be the ring-leader here. She was sitting on the piano belting a touching rendition of *Tomorrow* from the Annie Soundtrack. I rushed towards her and stopped directly in front of her. She had been staring out into space and suddenly recoiled upon seeing me in her space. She faltered then stopped singing abruptly.

"What's wrong?" she asked, scooting off the piano and placing a hand on my shoulder.

"What's wrong is that I can never stay here long enough to get any information, and when I wake up, I've forgotten it all!" I replied in a near shriek.

She nodded in understanding. "Yes, I can see the difficulty. That's because you have not yet Awoken."

"Then can somebody wake me up? And also, is there any way of arriving directly in this room? I keep arriving at various points outside, and it takes forever to make my way here. Once I made it as far as the back door, and the last time I made it to the elevator," I said, frustrated.

"I see," she said calmly, and I wanted to shake her. I whipped around, searching for the Teacher, but she wasn't in the room. "I can't awaken you, but I can help you stay here longer."

I gave her my best 'get on with it' stare, and she continued, "repeat after me. 'I wish to stay at the Castle for as long as is required to achieve my goal.'" She smiled brightly, proud to be of service. This one could give me lessons on calm and chipperness. I took a deep breath and repeated the sentence. I waited for a bit, but nothing happened.

"How do I know it worked?" I asked, impatient.

"You'll have to take my word for it," she replied and pulled me toward the sofa where Needlepoint was sitting contentedly stitching and humming, though no music was currently playing. I nodded at her and she gave me a serene smile. She would be my go-to for patience and serenity.

Singer and I sat opposite each other, she on the sofa and I in one of the armchairs.

"Tomorrow night, before you go to bed, you should say the phrase I just gave you along with 'I wish to go to the yellow sitting room' and 'I wish to remember all about my visit to the Castle.' That should solve your immediate problems," she said.

Just then, the Teacher appeared from the door and asked me to follow her. I shrugged and waved at Singer and Needlepoint. She led me down the hall to the elevator I had seen earlier that day. This must be a recent addition. I was pretty sure medieval castles didn't have elevators. On the way down, I told her about my conversation with Singer.

She nodded in approval. "Yes, you should be able to stay longer today. Especially since our goal is to hasten your Awakening," she replied.

The door dinged and we exited the elevator in what had to had been the dungeons once. Though the hall was well lit and the stone wall was clean, there was an unmistakable dampness to the air. It was cooler here than above, and I shivered slightly. As I followed her down the hallway, I wondered if I could conjure a sweater, when my favorite hoodie appeared in my hands.

At my astonished look, the Teacher chuckled. "You have much to learn," she said and stopped in front of a door. It was a smaller version of the carriage door, with a small opening. There were bars in the opening and I couldn't help but think that this led to an isolation chamber and take an involuntary step back.

"Don't worry, it's just an office," she said and pulled the door open. It wasn't locked. She led the way and turned on an overhead light. The room inside looked like a regular office, except that the back wall was a floor-to-ceiling aquarium. The Teacher motioned for me to sit in one of the armchairs in front of the fire, opposite the aquarium. I couldn't help turning and asking, "is that real?"

She chuckled. "No, it's an illusion. I don't choose the location of my office, but I have total control over how it appears. I like the ocean. Would you prefer another view?"

"No, that's fine," I replied and turned back towards the fireplace. The warmth of the fire pushed out the damp chill, and soon after, I took off my hoodie.

"Now, then. Let's begin. I'm sure you have many questions," she said and paused to let me ask them.

"I do. Yesterday, you told me you needed my help, but you never told me with what. I'm assuming that is why the goal is to hasten my

Awakening. Second, if this hadn't happened, when would I normally have Awakened? Third, what exactly does an Awakening entail?" I asked. *There, that about covers it.*

She studied me for a moment, perhaps wondering where to begin. Finally, she nodded to herself and said, "the Awakening happens when we are aware that we are creating our own reality. A moment ago, I told you I could control my office's appearance but not its location. It's the same in your life."

To demonstrate her point, she closed her eyes, and the office walls turned clear as glass. The office appeared to have been placed in the middle of the desert. I swiveled in my chair to take it in. When she spoke again, the room reverted to its previous appearance.

"You can control what happens in your life," she said.

"You mean I can change it as easily as you just did? Or do you mean that my life is actually an illusion?" I asked, unsure where she was going with this.

"Have you made something happen while in a dream?" she asked.

"Yes, I can change what I'm wearing or, if I don't like the dream, I can dream of something else," I replied.

"That's what we call lucid dreaming. It means that you are aware that you are dreaming and therefore can exert your will on what is going on. It's the same for your waking life, except it's not quite as instant. It requires a little more thought and skill," she answered.

"The Awakening is when you become aware of this in your waking life. Once that step is achieved, you can learn how to do it right here at the Castle. The first thing you learn is how to come here deliberately, in your waking hours."

"Wait, are you saying I can do magic? Close my eyes and make it so I'm at the beach or have an ice cream sundae appear before me?" I asked, half joking and half hopeful.

She laughed. "Perhaps, in time, with practice and determination, you could achieve those things. But for now, let's focus on letting you stay here long enough to learn something and be able to come here when you need answers."

"Does it involve a lot of meditation?" I asked, uneasy. I knew meditation would do me good, especially as I was such a worrier. But anything that begun with meditation was bound to take forever and yield very little.

"Meditation certainly helps, but no. I'm referring to being aware of your thoughts and the results they produce. Thoughts manifest into things. For example, every time you worry about something, you are calling that very thing to you," she explained.

"Is that why I'm not getting the grades I want in math and science?" I asked.

"It is very likely. Are you constantly afraid you might fail?" she asked.

"Yes! Or I'll have a poor grade," I wailed.

"There you go!" she said, waving her arms to mean she rested her case.

I mulled this over. Could it really be that simple?

At my skeptical expression, the Teacher said, "why don't you test it out, scientifically? Be sure to have a positive hypothesis, though. If you don't expect it to work, it can't work. Why do you think scientists get varying results from the same experiments? Because their expectations vary and are almost always confirmed!" she exclaimed with a grin.

I nodded, taking it in. *How can I test this?* I could expect to get an A on my next physics test. I was going to study for it anyway, and an A was what I wanted, but I never actually expected it.

"Ok, here is my hypothesis: I expect to get an A in my next Physics exam," I asserted.

"You've got to believe it's possible," she added.

"I'm attentive in class, take copious notes, do all the exercises, and study like my life depends on it. I should be getting As. I can't explain why I'm getting them until now. It's definitely more than possible," I said, excited now at the opportunities ahead.

"I'm going to ask you to close your eyes and imagine getting your exam back with a bright red A on it," she said. I closed my eyes.

In my mind, I was sitting in class as the teacher was passing out the graded exams. Instead of the usual dread I felt, I forced myself to feel an excited expectancy. I started to wiggle in my seat and silently clapping my hands in anticipation. When the teacher reached me, she was smiling and said, "I don't know what you did, but keep it up, kiddo!"

I thanked her and stared at my perfect grade. There was a warmth spreading in my chest, and the pressure was building. It's rising to my throat, and I couldn't help shouting, "woohoo!"

I realized then that I was, in fact, in the teacher's office, standing with a triumphant arm raised and a goofy grin on my face.

"Well done, Clare. If you can do that every day until your exam, I guarantee you'll see improvement," she said. "And do remember to repeat those phrases before bed tomorrow."

"Is it time to go already?" I asked. I was pumped. I was ready for the big stuff. "Wait, you still haven't told me what you need my help for?" I asked, but I could hear the insistent buzzing of my alarm clock.

CHAPTER SEVEN

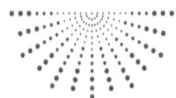

MIRACLE OF MIRACLES, AS I WOKE UP, I COULD REMEMBER EVERYTHING that happened at the Castle since I first went. Humans really were highly suggestible beings. This put a spring in my step because it meant that I was probably going to get an A in my physics exam. This was so exciting! I had to get out of bed.

A quick scroll through my social media showed no urgent posts or messages. I checked my planner and looked for things I could expect to do better at than I had in the past. I saw nothing pressing, other than it was a Thursday.

Mom picked me up from school as we went out to lunch with Nana every week, when she's around. Nana lived in a home for active seniors. That's not a euphemism. The place was amazing. It had a gym, an indoor pool with a hot tub and a sauna, a full-service restaurant that offered room service, a cafe with an outdoor patio, an outdoor pool and hot tub, two tennis courts, and it was right off the golf course. Nana was never home. She was either using the on-site amenities, participating in group classes and excursions, or travelling to exotic destinations.

I wanted to have Nana's life when I was older! Heck, I'd like to get half as many things done in a day as she did. Today, she was telling us about an eighteen-day tour of Morocco she registered for. It left in a week. It started in Casablanca and ended in Marrakesh, and included a ride through the desert on camelback. Mom was a little worried, but Nana told her it's a seniors' tour. What could go wrong? Indeed. The truth was Nana always had amazing trips and nothing ever went wrong other than the occasional delayed luggage.

My grandmother was loaded. She could afford first-class every-thing and she was taking advantage of it. It wasn't always like this. She and Grandad had a restaurant here in town and it had kept them very busy. When he had died, Nana couldn't imagine spending her days there without him. Neither Mom nor Uncle Riley—he was a big city lawyer—had wanted anything to do with it.

When an offer had come, she had taken it. It was worth a lot more than what they had estimated, mostly because it had been on land a developer had been eyeing for a bigger project. She had felt bad for the employees who would likely lose their jobs, but the developer had said it would take another year before he needed to close it down. He had promised to relocate the employees to his other businesses if they wanted.

That had settled and she had promptly put the house on the market. It had been too much upkeep and there had been too many reminders of Grandad. It too had sold quickly. It was the perfect house for a family, near a school and a playground and large enough to accommodate three or four kids.

With the restaurant, Nana and Granddad had hardly ever taken vacations. They had been chained to it, often working seven days a week once Mom and Riley had been off to college. You would think they would have worked less as they got older, but they had said it was their baby, the one that would never leave them.

I had never complained about it because, in addition to paying for Mom's and Riley's educations, they had put money aside for mine and my cousins'. Riley's kids were older than me. Chase was finishing high school this year and I heard he wanted to become a sports agent. He had the name for it. Evan was in his second year of law school. He planned to join his dad's firm. They did entertainment and sports law, very snazzy and very snooty. We weren't close.

When they dropped me off at school, Nana hugged me and squeezed a five-dollar bill in my hand with a wink. I winked back and slipped it into my jeans. Our little secret.

* * *

THE LAST TIME I HAD BEEN THIS EXCITED ABOUT GOING TO BED HAD been the night before Mom, Nana, and I had gone to Disney World together. It had been my first plane ride and the thought of seeing Ariel in person had made it really hard to fall asleep. I didn't have that problem now.

I spent the evening studying for the physics exam. Sam and I quizzed each other via video messaging for over an hour. We were ready. Before we logged off, I asked Sam, who always had good grades, if he expected to have good grades before an exam. He looked at me funny and said, "of course! Don't you?"

I stared at him, dumbstruck. Here I thought I had stumbled onto a magic ritual and he already knew about it. Maybe he was in on it? Cautiously, I asked, "how did you learn to do that?"

At first, he started laughing, but when he saw I was serious he replied, "gee, Clare, no one taught me. I just set a goal, do the work, and hope for the best."

Clearly, Sam didn't have bouts of self-doubt the way I did. At least, not about school. I decided to drop the matter and we said goodnight.

I was wiped from studying. I brushed my teeth, hugged mom goodnight, and crawled into bed. I forwent scrolling and instead repeated the words Singer told me to say: "'I wish to go to the yellow sitting room, to stay at the Castle for as long as is required to achieve my goal, to remember all about my visit."

CHAPTER EIGHT

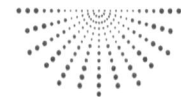

I ARRIVED BY THE FIREPLACE IN THE YELLOW ROOM, WHICH I HADN'T noticed on my previous visits. I was very pleased with myself. However, I soon realized that I was, in fact, alone in the room.

Heading for the door, I listened for sounds I could follow. When I heard nothing, I decided to test my new powers, so to speak. "I wish to be in Teacher's office," I said, eyes shut. I opened my eyes and saw I was now in the basement hall, staring at what seemed like an endless corridor of identical doors.

One of two things had happened. Either I couldn't enter the teacher's office without invitation or I was not specific enough as to which Teacher I wished to see. Considering there was an unlimited number of us, there had to be quite a few teachers.

But how could I specify which one I wanted to see? We were all the same! I decided to try something else. "I wish to speak with the Teacher who took me to her office yesterday, and who I met in the yellow room," I said. There, that should have been more specific.

I was still in the hall. It hadn't worked.

I was about to ask to see the fifteen-year-old Singer from the yellow room when I heard someone clearing their throat behind me. I whipped around and saw her. She was here! At least, I think that was her.

Smiling, she said, "well done, Clare. You made it here on your own. And you were able to call me. Excellent work. Shall we resume where we left off?" I nodded and smiled gratefully. I really didn't want to be alone down here. She opened the door next to us and motioned for me to precede her.

Now I was wondering if I had accidentally found the right door, or if all the doors would have led to her office, since she controlled it. I was also wondering where the others were. Not only the ones from the yellow room but any of the others. Other than the children I had seen in the courtyard, I hadn't crossed paths with anyone else yet.

"Now, then. You were asking why we need your help. I should say, your group needs you. Awakening means becoming aware of your power. Aware that you are not the victim of your circumstances. That you are the creator of everything you think, do, feel, see, hear, touch, taste, and smell. Once you are in your *knowing*, you are free from fear, doubt, or worry. Then you can create a wonderful life for yourself."

The more I listened, the warmer I felt in the center of my chest. If what she said was true, this was beyond magic. This was god-like power. "You mean like get good grades, win the lottery, get into a great college?" I asked, gauging how practical this could be or if it was just things like attaining inner peace. I mean, that would be great, but so would meeting a smart, cute guy.

She smiled and nodded. "Yes, that and so much more. Sometimes, we can't figure it out on our own and we come here. One of us can help. However, on our own, we cannot make important changes to the timeline or to major life events. We need more help. At your level of consciousness you need a group of twelve."

Strength in numbers. It made sense. "So, if one of us wants to change something major like save someone from a car accident, we could ask the others for help?" I asked.

"More or less. For now, you are restricted to things that are happening in your current calendar year."

"You mean we can go back or forward in time?" I asked, incredulously. She nodded. "But how? Is there a time machine?" I joked.

"Each girl in a group is attributed a different month of the year, as they Awaken. It usually coincides with the month that has recently completed in their reality. I believe it is April in your reality. You are therefore responsible for the month of March and can offer your perspective to the others in your group," she explained.

"But how can you be sure someone will awaken every month?" I asked, trying to figure this out.

"If two girls awaken the same month, they will be placed in different groups. A group is composed of twelve girls from alternate, but similar, realities. There might be millions of girls with similar realities. Those that are only slightly different are not placed together.

"Because you came to us, your life trajectory has now changed. This new you is here with us. The old you will continue to worry about everything and struggle with exams. When she Awakens, she will be placed in another group," she said.

"I see. I guess now I should stop thinking about the girls in terms of their skills but in terms of their month. So, the help that is needed, is it for the month of March or for something bigger?" I asked.

"As it happens, both," she replied. "However, I'm not yet at liberty to tell you what it is until you've mastered a few basic skills. You've already mastered the ability to remember your time here, choose a location, and call a Teacher or Guide to you. I'd like you now to call your group leader," she said.

"Is that Singer?" I asked and she chuckled.

"Yes, though you may use January to call her," she told me.

"Now?" I asked to be sure, and she nodded again. I closed my eyes and said, "I wish to see January."

When I opened my eyes, I expected her to be in the room with us. Instead, I was home sitting on the couch, snug under my blanket, reading the first chapter of *The Giver*. *Wait, what? I just finished it, why am I reading it again?* Then I noticed the pajamas I was wearing. These weren't mine. The bottoms were pink fleece with musical notes on them and the top was white and read 'Superstar.' Gag. This couldn't be right.

I flung off the blanket, discarded the book, and ran into the kitchen. Someone was making pancakes. The kitchen looked the same, except there was a man chopping berries. Who was this guy? Mom's boyfriend? Now I knew this wasn't right.

He saw me in the doorway and asked if I wanted whipped cream. Automatically, I replied "yes, please," as I made my way into the kitchen.

He nodded to the piano in the dining room and said, "will you play something for us? Breakfast is almost ready."

I looked over at the piano. It was a *real* piano. Mesmerized, I nodded and sat on the bench. There were sheets on the piano stand. The piece was called "Horseman Op. 27" by Dmitri Kabalevsky. I had no idea what that was. Nonetheless, I laid my hands on the keys and began.

My fingers were flying on the keys. It was an upbeat piece I'd expect to hear during a silent cowboy movie. It was over in under a minute. I was sure I nailed it and beamed as Mom and the photographer—whose name I somehow knew—applauded. I stood and took a bow as they brought plates to the dining room table. As soon as I sat down to eat, I was back in the Teacher's office, still in the armchair.

I shook my head. It boggled my mind that I could seamlessly move from one place to the next, or from one reality to another. I was expecting more fanfare, something like a rush of wind or a queasy feeling in my stomach. But it was really like changing channels on the TV.

"That was incredible!" I said, looking at my hands in amazement. "She's a good piano player. I wished I'd heard her sing. Or had time to eat those pancakes," I said, looking at the Teacher now. She was wearing her own astonished look and I frowned. "What?" I asked.

"When I asked you to call January, I expected you to call her here, not teleport yourself into her life. She was meant to explain how to do that," she exclaimed.

"Oh, sorry," I replied.

"No, don't apologize. That was very well done! You don't need to close your eyes and say it out loud. You can just think about it. But if it helps you focus, it's not a problem," she said in a reassuring tone. "Now, ask January to join us, in your mind this time," she said.

I called her up in my mind and she appeared. "What's up?" she asked and settled on the stool near the fireplace.

"Where were you, before you were here? Did you suddenly disappear, or did you hear me and choose whether or not to come?" I asked in fascination.

"In my reality, I'm asleep just like you. Part of me is dreaming, and another part of me is working with a Teacher on the third floor. She's giving me singing lessons," she stated.

I pointed to her sitting on the stool. "Is this another part of you or is it the same part of you that's singing on the third floor?" I asked.

I was still wrapping my brain around the concept of an infinite number of versions of me at various ages, living an infinite number of realities. I also kinda got that I could be home sleeping, yet here at the same time. But being here *and* in two other places at once was too much for my brain to process.

"Sorry, my mistake. I was doing vocal exercises when I heard your call. I excused myself and came here," she said, breaking it down for me.

"But it took you less than a nanosecond to do all that!" I exclaimed.

"It happens instantly. Remember, there is no time here. Everything happens at the same time, past, present, and future," answered the Teacher.

"What if I call you, either of you, when I'm awake? What would happen then?" I asked.

"That's a little more advanced, but it's similar to what you experienced when you asked to see January. The one being called would embody your experience," said the teacher.

"Like a body snatcher?" I asked in horror.

January burst out laughing. "No, silly. Like a guest in your head. If you called me to ask for advice on something, you would hear it in your mind. If you needed me to sing in your place, for example, then I'd have to take over, obviously."

My eyes were wide like saucers. "You could take over and do stuff for me? Like, take my physics exam, for example?" I asked, imagining the possibilities.

"Well you wouldn't want me to do that, I'm probably worse at it than you are. But technically, yes. But we'd both have to agree. I couldn't take over without your consent and you couldn't make me do it against my will."

This was incredible. My brain was on overload trying to figure out the ramifications of what had just been said.

"That's why the girls in our group have different skills!" I exclaimed, grinning. My face fell when I realized I had no skill to offer. What could they possibly want with me?

"Yes, and to show each of you that you can literally do anything you set your mind to. The sky's the limit, so to speak," put in the Teacher.

"I don't have any skills. Not like January. Can I call you January?" I asked her belatedly.

"Yes, March," she replied with a wink.

"Of course you have skills," the Teacher countered. "We all have our own unique gifts. You just don't know what yours are yet because you are still wracked with fear, doubt, and worry. You are blind to your strengths. Once you Awaken, you'll gain clarity and self-confidence."

"I can give you a clue, though," she said, smiling. "You excel at organization, analysis, and strategy. It's why you find so much to worry about, because you are always analyzing all the variables that could go wrong. Imagine if you used your gifts positively, for a change!"

She was trying to be encouraging, but I felt the sting of her words, nonetheless. My unworthiness was creeping to the surface, gripping my throat and pools formed in my eyes.

January looked at the teacher in alarm and rushed to wrap me up in a hug. "Don't feel bad, most people feel that way, all the time. You get a chance to change things and make them better. That's all the Teacher is saying."

The Teacher left her chair to crouch near my chair and stroke my hair. "You are going to achieve great things. Do you know how I know?" she asked soothingly. I sniffled and shook my head.

"Because I am a version of this new you from the future," she said with a wink.

CHAPTER NINE

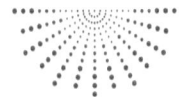

I woke up longing to visit my life in the future and resisted the urge to call the Teacher. I didn't have time. It was exam day. I flew through my morning routine and headed straight to class when I arrived at school, instead of meeting my friends near our lockers.

I needed to stay focused. The door was unlocked, and the room was empty. Perfect! I headed for my seat, arranged my pens, calculator, a bottle of water, and tissues neatly on my desk and placed the rest of my things under my seat.

Normally, I would cram during these precious last minutes, but now I closed my eyes and called up the vision I had in the Teacher's office. In minutes, I was overcome with joy, like I ate sunshine and drank a rainbow. I was feeling like I was suntanning in the backyard. The light was bright behind my eyelids and a beam was hitting me straight through the heart.

Someone nudged me on the way to their seat and a cloud moved in front of the sun. I blinked back to reality. I no longer felt as high as I had, but I was still wearing a goofy grin. I was going to nail this exam.

I turned to look at Sam. He was staring at me with an unreadable expression. I gave him a thumbs-up, still grinning, and his response was a raised eyebrow and an amused smile. I turned back. The teacher had placed the exam in front of me. I took a deep breath, grabbed my pen, and waited for the signal to begin.

I read through all the questions and highlighted important facts. I didn't need to start with the easier questions, they were all easy! Or at the very least, the answers came easily. I made my way through the booklet, read over each of my answers twice, and put my pen down. Checking that I had written my name and group number, I raised my hand to signal that I was finished. The teacher cocked his head and looked at the clock. I had completed a seventy-five-minute exam in thirty minutes. We were both shocked. I usually was the one who asked for extra time.

He motioned for me to bring my booklet but put a hand up to keep me from going back to my seat. He flipped through the booklet to ensure I hadn't forgotten any questions. Looking up, he pointed a thumb at the board behind him. He had written the chapters to do as homework. I nodded and headed back to my seat as quietly as I could. I felt like skipping.

I was engrossed in my physics notebook and neither saw nor heard the teacher approach me. I jumped at the sight of him. He was holding my exam. My graded exam! His face was neutral, I couldn't tell if it was good or bad. He didn't hold me in suspense for long. He placed a finger on his mouth to remind me to stay quiet as students were still working on their own exams, though many had finished already.

It happened just like in my vision. His arm lowered in slow motion as he handed me the exam. Not only did I have a good grade, I had a perfect grade. He had scrawled a huge "100%" with a red sharpie followed by four exclamation points and a happy face. I looked up, tears welling in my eyes. I mouthed the words 'thank you' as I cradled the test to my chest. He smiled and mouthed back, 'it's all you.' He held out his hand, he wanted the test back. I looked at it one more time, sighed with happiness, and reluctantly handed it back to him.

When the bell rang, Sam dropped his booklet on the teacher's desk and waited for me outside the classroom. When I walked out, he pulled me into a hug.

"I saw your grade, that's amazing Clare. I knew you had it in you!" he said as he released me.

I beamed with pride and replied, "I'm sure you did well, too."

He shrugged and said, "of course!" He nodded towards the hallway and said, "come on, I'll walk you to your next class and you can tell me how you did it."

* * *

IN FRENCH CLASS, MONSIEUR MARCEL HANDED OUT OUR GRADED responses. He had given me a ninety-six percent and written 'Bravo!' I had a few grammar errors and forgot to add a title. Regardless, it was the best French grade I had ever had on a written assignment.

My joy was short-lived. We needed to prepare a short oral presentation based on our written response. I bowed my head in desperation. I perked up when I heard he'd be listening to our responses individually, out in the hall. My heart leapt and I couldn't resist clapping. I was immediately mortified when everyone turned and looked at me.

We had fifteen minutes to practice in pairs and Monsieur Marcel told us to be prepared to answer follow-up questions.

I paired up with Joshua. He was the least judgy of the bilinguals. He lived on my street and we went to elementary school together, but we were not friends. He was in the robotics program and, well, still spent his time playing with plastic bricks. But he made a good partner since we had nothing personal to talk about to distract us from the task at hand.

When it was my turn, I took a moment before going out in the hall to apply what I had learned at the Castle. *I can do this.* Monsieur Marcel started by saying how pleased he was with my progress in class. This bolstered my confidence and I started my comments on *Barbe Bleue* with excitement. He asked about women's traditional roles in the home, and about gender dynamics in today's relationships. I took my time and all the words I needed were instantly available to me. I realized my accent was not as pronounced as I had imagined.

The teacher nodded as I spoke and scribbled furiously on his notepad. Minutes later, he showed me the grid; it read ninety-two percent. I was so happy, I didn't even look at my errors. I just didn't care. Besides, he'd scan it and post it to the parents' portal. "Merci, Monsieur Marcel," I stammered out, still reeling from my accomplishment.

I felt like jumping from joy, but I had already clapped like a lunatic today. I went back to class and called the next student. On my way back to my seat, I checked the whiteboard for our next assignment. We needed to choose from among the novels in the bookcase and the corresponding study unit.

Lo and behold, a translation of *The Giver* was one of the choices. I quickly grabbed a copy of the book and grabbed the unit from the cabinet. Could this day get any better?

Actually, it could. After a quick lunch, I headed for the Language Arts class for my tutoring gig. I was on time, but my student was not. I asked the teacher what to do and she said to wait another five minutes and if he didn't show up, I could leave.

He never showed up. I still got paid. Sweet! I debated looking for my friends or going for a walk. It was a gorgeous spring day and most students were out in shirt sleeves. Walking it was. It was too nice to walk in the tiny woods behind the school, and the grass was too soggy to walk on. I followed the path that led to the pool and found a perfectly positioned bench to sit on and soak up some rays.

I sat there in total bliss until the bell rang, and then I headed back to class. I felt like a superstar.

CHAPTER TEN

I was talking a mile a minute and Mom was listening with an indulgent smile. When I finally came up for air, she said, "I'm so proud of you, honey. You're finally coming into your own!" I cringed at the last part. Such a mom thing to say. I focused on her pride. It didn't make me feel as joyful as it usually did. Or I should say, not as much as how proud of myself I felt. I swished this new feeling in my mouth and swallowed the ambrosia.

Mom had picked up pastries for dessert. It's our Friday night splurge. There was a selection of bite-sized classics to choose from. I picked an almond tart and a mille-feuille. Mom had an eclair and a tiramisu. We savored these with a cup of our favorite rooibos and vanilla tea while we decided what movie to watch after dinner.

We settled on the new adaptation of Little Women and planned to meet in the living room at seven-thirty. Mom's friend Michelle was early for their walk so I offered to do the dishes by myself. She kissed me on the forehead and promised to be back in an hour.

I pulled up my music playlist and sent it to our smart speaker system. It would keep me company as I cleaned up the kitchen. I took advantage of having the place to myself and showed off my dance moves and my lack of singing ability.

I was right in the middle of belting an 80s classic when I heard, "you're not a bad singer!" I screeched to a halt, my arms barely still flailing about. I looked at the front door, no Mom. Back door, nothing. I told to the smart speaker to can it and listen. The windows were closed, it was not coming from outside.

"Is now a good time?" the voice asked. It was coming from inside my head, I realized.

"Who is this?" I asked out loud. There was no response. I repeated my question in my head.

"It's January. Can you come to the Castle?" she asked.

I checked the time on the oven clock. It was only six-thirty. Mom wouldn't be back for at least another thirty minutes, maybe an hour if the gossip was good. "Sure, give me a minute," I replied. I went to my room, closed the door, and laid on my bed. If Mom would knock and not get a reply, she'd think I was napping.

I said my usual intentions and arrived just inside the door of the yellow room. January was sitting on the sofa with a serious-looking girl wearing the kind of clothes my mom wore for work: navy pleated pants, a white shirt, and a maroon jacket.

As I sat, I saw there was a crest on the breast pocket of the jacket. She was on the debate team. Maybe she was just back from a regional meet. Her hair was pulled back in a severe bun. She wore no makeup, her unvarnished nails were clipped short, and the only jewelry I saw on her was the watch Nana gave us last Christmas.

She extended her hand, all business-like. "Hi, I'm April." I shook it and told her I was March, but she already knew that. January asked if I wanted tea or coffee. I declined. Was I finally going to know what's going on?

"Well done on your Physics test!" she said. I narrowed my eyes at her, about to ask how she knew, but she was April. She knew everything that happened in April in all twelve of our realities.

"Thanks," I replied politely.

January took over the conversation. "Right. Now that you've mastered the basic skills, it's time to get down to business. At present, you know what happens in March of your reality, but not the other realities. That's what you'll be working on this weekend. But as the matter is rather urgent, April is going to share what's been going on in her reality for the past few weeks."

"When you say share, do you mean we're going to talk about it, or do you mean I'm going to visit her life the way I did yours?" I asked. January's life was amazing, but I wasn't so sure I wanted to see April's life. From the look of her, she had no fun whatsoever. I berated myself immediately as I realized that by judging her life, I was judging myself.

"I'll take you back through a series of key memories. You won't be acting *as* me, just going along for the ride, so to speak," explained April.

I shrugged and said, "Let's go!" She took my hand and I was immediately back in my room, studying for the math test I failed miserably a few days ago. The room was different. For one thing, it was a lot tidier than mine. I checked my planner and saw it was packed with afterschool activities and weekend outings. Where did she find the time?

Mom called out to tell me Sam was here. Sam? We usually studied remotely, it was more efficient. Frowning, I opened my door and there he was, reaching for the handle. I didn't have time to check out the kitchen and look for differences because Sam's hand snaked around my waist and pulled me close as he kissed me full on the lips. On. The. Lips. *What?*

"In the dining room guys, you know the rules!" hollered mom from the living room. Sam grabbed the books from my desk and took them to the dining room table where he dropped his backpack.

I grabbed a couple bottles of mineral water from the fridge and joined him at the table. I was not driving this body, so I could only observe. However, I could feel what April felt. This was a regular occurrence. Kissing him was pleasant and natural, not first-kiss thrilling. *Me and Sam?* It boggled the mind. Sure, we had been best friends since grade school, but that was it.

The scene changed. I was watching a Barbie movie with a girl about nine years old in the living room. It was Penny, my baby sister, and we were snuggling under a blanket. I had a sister in this reality? Who's her dad?

There was no time to ask because the scene changed again. We're in some kind of waiting room. Everything was institutional grey, but it didn't feel like a hospital. Other people were waiting, talking in low voices.

There was a huge buzzing sound, like being buzzed into an office building but louder. My eyes followed the sound to a speaker right next to the clock. It was ten o'clock and the large steel door opened automatically.

Families filed in through the door. Sam said, "are you ready?" and I nodded. We followed the others into a large cafeteria-like room, with the type of round metal picnic tables where the seats were attached. There was a man sitting at each table, waiting for his visitors. *Oh my God!* We're visiting someone in prison. Who? Why?

We reached our destination and there was Dad. Wait, *Dad?* He wrapped me in a tight hug. April hugged him back, she was happy to see him. He released me and shook Sam's hand. "I'll be in the waiting room if you need me," he said and kissed my cheek before he left. Dad motioned for me to sit.

He didn't look the way I remembered him from the pictures. I had never met him. Mom had said he had died when I was a baby. He looked older, leaner, and tan. Like he spent a lot of time outdoors. He was smiling at me, hands clasped on the table.

I was still drinking him in when we came back to the yellow room. I had a ton of questions. I opened my mouth, but January held up her hand to stop me. "You'll get all the details tonight," she said. "We just needed you to understand the situation before we proceed."

"Dad is a corporate banker. He's been charged with embezzling company funds," said April.

"Did he do it?" I asked.

CHAPTER ELEVEN

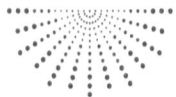

M OM AND HER FRIEND WERE BACK AND CHATTING IN THE DOORWAY, making plans to have lunch next week. I was still reeling from April's revelations. Did Mom lie about Dad being dead or did he just not die in April's reality? Could I go back in time and change things so that he would be alive in mine? Was Dad a crook? Had he been a crook back then? Had he been in jail this whole time?

I heard Mom coming. I sat up and grabbed a book, pretending to read. "Ready for the movie?" she asked. "I'm making popcorn!"

I wanted to ask her about Dad. Instead, I said, "in a minute," with false cheer. I had never felt less like watching a movie. I wanted to pick at this scab until the pus came out. I tossed the book, squared my shoulders, and practiced patience. All would be revealed tonight.

The movie was good, but it was a tearjerker that had us blubbering. Tonight, I would have preferred a comedy to distract me. I kept telling myself that what was happening to April was not happening to me. I *felt* like it was, though.

When the movie ended, we brushed our teeth and said goodnight. I reminded myself that the only thing I could do was to expect the best possible outcome. But what would that look like? Clearly, something had happened in March that April thought could be avoided or handled differently.

I said the words, they were part of my nightly routine now. I was not sure I still needed them, but they helped me focus. Especially since my mind was so agitated with worry. I slowed my breathing. In for five counts, out for five counts.

When I got to the yellow room, January and April were waiting for me. There were other girls in the room, chatting in low voices by the window. As I took my seat on the sofa, the teacher appeared at the door and soon joined us.

"April, have you had a chance to speak with your Guide?" she asked. My ears perked up. This was the first time anyone had referred to the Guides.

"Yes, she said that I need to gather information from the past three months to assess where the problem originated. I've already spoken to January and February. Once I have March's perspective, I'll be able to proceed," replied April.

"Proceed how?" I asked. I wanted to know how this worked. If it was guaranteed to work.

"Once April has all the facts—well from her perspective, since she'll never know the facts from anyone else's perspective, like your parents for example—she'll put in a request to speak with herself in the future. Should the events play out without interference, what would be the outcome? Depending on the gravity of the situation, you may speak with up to five future versions of yourself. If you cannot accept the outcomes, you may petition for a reality adjustment. That's when you explain what you want to your group. If everyone agrees, the adjustment is performed," explained the Teacher.

I was trying to wrap my brain around meeting various future versions of myself. Was one of them my Guide? Did my Guide change every time I made a decision?

"Why does everyone need to agree? Why would someone disagree?" I asked.

January fielded this question. "Technically, the only reason someone would disagree is if the changes you are requesting would cause harm to you or someone else."

"Or if the change eliminates an important outcome. When you meet to discuss the petition, you'll receive the perspectives of the girls responsible for the months after the event. This will give you the short-term outcome of the unchanged event," put in the Teacher.

"Can you give me an example?" I said. I was confused.

"Let's say what you wanted was to prevent a breakup between you and your boyfriend. But June tells you that you've met an even better guy. She would disagree with your request," explained April.

"Oh, I guess that makes sense. But what if I really pleaded my case?" I asked.

"If you are not doing yourself or others any harm, whoever had objections could go your way. You would obviously be trying to learn something through the experience," answered January.

I found this answer satisfactory. Unless I had evil intentions, my petition would likely be approved. Evil. "There has to be evil, or naughty versions of me, right. To keep the balance?" I asked.

"Yes, but they are not here. This is Clarity Castle, home to those seeking clarity," replied the Teacher.

"Do they have their own place, like, Obscurity Castle?" I snorted. Everyone laughed at this.

"No, dear. And there is no in-between either, in case you were about to ask. There is no darkness, only the absence of light. There-fore, the versions who are not here at the Castle are either on their way or are not following their path to clarity," she explained.

"But what if I did something very naughty, like rob a bank?" I asked.

"Do you remember that scene in the movie *Legally Blonde* where Elle insists that Brooke is innocent by stating *'exercise gives you endorphins. Endorphins make you happy. Happy people just don't shoot their husbands?'*" said January in a perfect imitation of Reese Whiterspoon's character. I grinned. We all did. It's one of our favorite movies.

"Are you saying that if I was happy, I wouldn't rob a bank?" I asked.

"Exactly! Happiness is not just a feeling, it's also a frequency. The higher the frequency, the better you feel. At higher frequencies, you have access to different thoughts and experiences. If you had a problem, you could ask any one of us to help you solve it easily," added April.

"What do you mean by frequencies? Like on the radio?" I asked.

"Yes, just like on the radio. If you are tuned into the happy channel, you can only hear happy music. If you are tuned into the grumpy channel, you can imagine what you'll hear," she said.

I mulled this over. The channel I tuned into the most was the worry channel. That would mean I heard worrisome music, or rather thoughts and experiences. That was probably why I stayed stuck there.

"But how do you change the channel?" I asked.

"By distracting yourself. The point is to stop thinking whatever thought as you tuned in. It's very hard to change your thoughts at first. It's best to simply focus elsewhere entirely. The best ways are to take a nap, meditate, go for a walk, listen to some music, play with your pet, or do anything that brings you joy. You'll quickly change the channel. In the case of nap or meditation, you'd be turning off the radio altogether," explained January.

I nodded, understanding. "When I came here the first time, I was walking off a bad mood. You're saying that as soon as I let go of being disappointed about my grade, I changed the channel. Does the Castle have its own channel?" I asked.

"Not exactly," replied the teacher. "Imagine if you will a thermometer, where zero degrees are a neutral temperature, or frequency in our case. As the frequency rises, the feelings are positive. If it drops, the feelings are negative. The feelings just above zero are contentment or satisfaction, optimism, and enthusiasm, rising all the way up to joy. Just below, you'll find boredom, worry, and anger, dropping all the way down to fear.

"There are many feelings in between. To see all of them, simply look up the emotional scale online when you're back in your world.

Anyhow, the moment you rise above zero, you can access the Castle and all of us," explained the teacher.

It sounded easy enough. "Is it possible to stay above zero all the time?" I asked.

"Only if you stay here. Life on Earth isn't meant to be perfect. It's meant to be real and unique. You get to choose what happens, moment to moment. Most people choose unconsciously, through habits of thought. It seems like life is happening to them, that they are powerless. If they are tuned into the powerless station..." said the teacher.

"All they get are powerless thoughts and experiences," I exclaimed as the scope of the implication sank in.

This was huge. It explained January's seemingly charmed life. She was always chipper and passionate. I looked at her closely, then at April. January's skin was flawless, her hair was glossy, her eyes bright. I could feel the joy seeping out of her. It felt warm, inviting. April, on the other hand, looked like someone applied a matte filter to her. She was not dull, but even when she smiled, the wattage seemed dimmer. I didn't feel a pull towards her, but I didn't feel repelled by her either. I felt comfortable in her presence. It occurred to me that my own frequency was probably matching hers. I smiled at her, a wave of compassion coming over me. She smiled back.

The teacher beamed at us. "Both of your frequencies just rose!" We all beamed back.

"It's almost time to go. Do you have any more questions about frequencies?" asked January.

"No, I get it. It's pretty straightforward. What I really want to know is how I'll access information about other realities. You said I'm responsible for the month of March. I know what happens in my life, and I've got a few clues about April's recent events. How do I get the rest of it?" I asked.

"That's the fun part! You'll spend a month in each reality—as a visitor, of course," put in January.

"A month! You mean I'll live the whole month of March as each of the other eleven girls that are in our group? Won't that take forever?" I exclaimed.

"You forget that we are outside of time and space. You could literally spend a year here and go back to your life tomorrow morning when you wake up," replied April.

That was intense. It also meant I could visit or try out any number of lives.

"If we can visit our other realities, why do we need to go back and change something? Wouldn't it be easier to look into it here in advance?" I asked.

"Yes, it would. Right now, you imagine you'll come here every night and check out all the possible scenarios and choose the best ones. However, eventually, you'll focus on something else and it won't be a priority. Or your frequency will drop for a while. Later, you might even learn the value of strife," said the Teacher.

"The value of strife?" I asked.

"Yes. Solving problems, overcoming obstacles, or achieving goals is satisfying. It feels good. If nothing ever happens to rock the boat, it's easy to fall into boredom. Food always tastes better when you're hungry," explained January.

It all made sense. It was like a game. Sometimes you won, sometimes you lost. But you kept playing, striving for victory.

"What happens if I like another reality better than mine?" I asked as the thought occurred to me.

"For now, we need you to commit to viewing all eleven realities. Should you truly prefer one of the other realities, you could simply pop into it and continue from there," replied the Teacher.

"But what would happen to mine? What about the other girl who's already living it?" I asked.

"Your reality would continue as March. Your consciousness would merge with the other girl's. Let's say it was mine. You and I would identify as January, but there would only be one of us," explained January.

It was giving me a headache but I got it.

"Bear in mind that it is highly unlikely that you will prefer a different reality. You will probably like different things about each reality and wish to integrate them into your own," added April. I nodded. We all nodded.

"Are you ready?" asked January, holding out a hand to me.

I hesitated a moment, then grabbed her hand. It was January, I was sure I would have a great time.

CHAPTER TWELVE

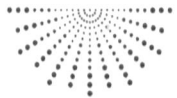

"Remember, Clare. You call me if there's a problem, and I'll come and get you," said Mom, hugging me really tight. She was misty-eyed as she stroked my hair and put her hands on either side of my face. She was acting as if she'd never see me again.

"It's just for a week, Mom," I replied, hands on her shoulders. "I'll be fine." I looked to Gary for help.

"Come on, honey. We're cramping her style. Can't you see all her musician friends are waiting for her to ditch her parents?" He gave me a quick hug and pulled Mom towards the car. "See you next Sunday at four."

I waved at them and headed towards my friends—or I should say, January's friends. She would be spending March break at Bandcamp. I cringed, dreading a week filled with organized group activities, and all musical, no less. January was stoked. So were the giggling girls who greeted me. I knew their names. Marisol played the piano, Allegra played the cello, and Daphne was a soprano singer like me, um, like January.

Once the hugging and rejoicing were dispensed with, we headed for our dorm room and claimed the bunks. I got a top bunk, yes! I unpacked the things I'd need for tonight and plugged in my phone. This wasn't my first time at camp.

During the school year, I was registered in the music-study program. Three afternoons per week, I received private lessons here at the Music Academy in Orford. I spent a week here for March break and four weeks in the summer.

As soon as I finished high school, I'd be able to audition for gigs or talent shows. My coach had been hounding Mom for years, but she wanted me to focus on my studies. She was not wrong. If I got a spot on a show or in a band, I'd drop everything.

I was amazed that January had such good grades despite having to condense her time at school and spend so many hours per week practicing her singing and the piano. I was also surprised that I was so chatty.

We were in a co-ed common room with a bunch of other kids. I recognized some of them from school. It was like a party. I looked around the room and saw that two adults were sitting on bar stools in a makeshift kitchen. Presumably instructors. They too were chatting animatedly, ignoring their charges.

I got why everyone's excited. We would be spending a week together, without parents, and loosely supervised. Some kids started playing card games and board games, others were jamming and singing acapella. I tuned out for a while.

These were January's friends and this was her scene. It felt completely alien to me, but I could see myself living this life. I remembered when I was a kid, I was always singing. A friend of Mom's had given us her upright piano because it wouldn't fit in her new apartment. I took lessons for a while, but I couldn't be bothered to practice. Mom eventually sold the piano.

At ten o'clock, our minders sent us off to bed. Classes started at eight, breakfast was at seven. So much for a week off.

The week actually flew by, and I admit I enjoyed it. My favorite part was the daily duet rehearsals with Etienne. He was a sixteen-year-old hottie who went to one of the French private schools. He's not a French-speaking student, he's actually French. He spoke with an adorable Parisian accent, but he sang in perfect English. It boggled the mind.

January liked his smoky grey eyes and his jet-black hair. Those were great. What got me was his ramrod posture and the fact that his breath was always minty fresh. We had to sing in the same microphone in a rather small booth. There was only room enough for a single music holder. Every day, we stood shoulder to shoulder for thirty minutes, sharing the same air while singing Italian arias from the opera *Don Giovani*.

There was a concert on Sunday and we totally nailed it. Our rendition of *Là ci darem la mano* yielded us a standing ovation. I was so proud I could burst. Standing on that stage, Etienne squeezing my hand tightly, felt like the whole world was loving me.

We took our bow and exited stage left. As overcome with emotion as I was, there were a number of equally appreciable performances during the show.

Backstage, Etienne and I hugged quickly and he was talking a mile a minute in French. I got that he was happy we nailed it. The voice coach sent us an Italian 'Bellissimo' kiss as he ushered out the next duet.

The final number had the whole ensemble singing *September* by Earth, Wind and Fire. It's a great number, all the parents were clapping. When the show was over, the parents had cocktails and chatted with the faculty while the kids cleaned up. By five, everyone had tearfully gone back to their daily lives.

Gary took Mom and me out for dinner to celebrate. We talked about our week and January shared that she might like to learn Italian. I rolled my eyes. How was she going to fit that in? Mom thought it was a fabulous idea, especially since I did so well in the duet. For Mom, having me perform opera would be a sight better than being in a pop band. Gary just winked at me.

Gary's so chill. Nothing ever phased him. I felt guilty admitting this to myself, but I liked him better than Mom in this reality. Where

Mom was saying *'go, go, go,'* he's saying *'take it one day at a time.'* It's a nice balance.

The following week, I got to experience January's daily life. Every day, she was up at six. She drank a huge glass of water, popped a probiotic, and headed out for a twenty-minute jog. She listened to classical music as she jogged.

Back at home, she did a quick yoga and stretching routine then sat in front of the patio door as she sipped a cup of hot water with lemon and honey. It's soothing, the drink and the staring.

Next was a shower, getting dressed for school, and breakfast with the parents. I searched her mind to figure out how long Gary's been around. Five years. I had been in grade school. They had met at a summer camp concert. He had been there taking pictures for a magazine profile on the Music Academy. He worked as a staff photographer for a company that published a dozen or so trade magazines. Because he also played the piano, he had been instrumental in January's artistic development.

After breakfast, I did ten minutes of vocal exercises in front of the mirror in my room, packed up my school bag and hopped on the bus. Monday, Wednesday, and Friday mornings, I had English Language Arts and math class, always with the same group.

There were two groups for the music-study program. The first was for those at the school's in-house music academy. It was a wind orchestra, and anyone could join, no musical ability required. The other group was for those of us with musical talent receiving instruction elsewhere. For the first three years of high school, most of us went to the regional Music Academy. For the last two years, the more promising students attended classes at the university in Montreal, if they could afford the tuition. Otherwise, they continued at the regional school.

As soon as the bell rang, we grabbed our lunch bags and headed for the bus that would take us to our afternoon music lessons. It was a thirty-minute drive and the only lunch break we had. It was pleasant enough. I sat with Marisol and we chatted about the usual: exams, music, and boys.

When we got to school, we were required to go for a twenty-minute silent walk on the trail that went around the campus. It occurred to me that this was our equivalent of the two weekly P.E. classes. I could get used to this.

Upon our return, we split up by instrument and by level. Daphne and I were joined by three other girls for the soprano group. We spent the afternoon together with our teacher, but each spent thirty minutes alone, in turn, with the voice coach.

At three-thirty, the bus took us back to school. We arrived just in time to hop on the bus heading home. I spent the fifteen-minute ride home listening to music and staring out the window. Though January was used to this and I could feel she was fine with it, I was mentally exhausted.

She jumped straight into the math and English Language Arts homework. We had dinner with the parents, then I headed back to my room to study. There's a science test the next day. Bedtime for January was similar to mine, except that instead of scrolling online before falling asleep, she read. For fun.

On Tuesdays and Thursdays, she had Science and French (second language, lucky duck!) in the morning and Math and English Language Arts in the afternoon. Social Studies had been integrated into the English Language Arts. Instead of enjoying her full lunch hour with friends, January spent it in her Math and Science teacher's class getting remediation or getting a jump on homework.

The next three weeks were more of the same. On weekends, her morning routine was the same. After breakfast, she hit the books. Saturday afternoons, she usually hung out with her friends. Half the time, they were studying.

On Sunday afternoons, she and her parents did outdoor activities like hiking or biking. Afterwards, they had dinner with Nana and her new boyfriend.

Friday nights, she snuggled under a blanket and caught up on the TV shows she had recorded, while Mom and Gary were out for date night. Saturday nights, they went out to dinner and went to the movies or got take-out and watched one at home.

It's a well-organized life and not devoid of fun. But it's not one I'd want to step into and take over. I was going to miss Gary though. I wondered if he'd pop up in another reality. Meanwhile, I thought I would dust off that midi keyboard and plug it into my computer. You never knew!

CHAPTER THIRTEEN

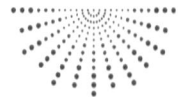

I was back in the yellow room with a head rush. There were more girls in the sitting room now. I wondered if I had been here the whole time or if I had blinked out while I was in January's memories and only now popped back. I was about to ask if I'd need to hold hands with February, when the Gymnast sat down beside me.

"How did it go? Are you ready for another?" asked the Teacher. In essence, I had just spent thirty days inside January's life, or her memories. The process was still a bit fuzzy. But I felt like barely five minutes had passed.

"It was great," I replied. Then, to January I said, "Gary's the best!" and she nodded with enthusiasm.

February held out her hands, a question in her eyes. I took a deep breath and took hold of them.

* * *

I was instantly transported to the Sunday before March Break. This time I was in the car with Mom and her friend, driving to a gymnastics club in Montreal. It was the Elite Canada Seniors' Competition and it was the first time February was competing as a Senior.

The event was the first of three annual competitions. The second was later in March and the last was in April.

Should she qualify, she'd go on to the Canadian Championships in May. If things went well, she could apply to be on the National Team. Though she doubted she'd make it that far on her first try, the next step was the World Artistic Gymnastics Championships in October.

February was best at bars, but she was required to compete in all four events, vault, bars, beam, and floor. Both she and her coach, which turned out to be Mom's friend, were pleased with her performance.

I was amazed at the strength and agility of this body. On the mat, I kept looking for a trampoline to justify the height of these jumps and flips, but there was none. She's got springs for legs. And she's so focused. It's loud and hectic in the gym during the competition, with two events happening at once and lots of cheering parents and team members. February blocked it all out. All I heard was her breathing. All I felt was calm determination.

To avoid going back and forth every day, we would be staying in a nearby hotel. This was how I learned that Mom and the coach were a couple. As I was digesting the fact that Mom was gay in this reality, it occurred to me that she might be gay in mine too. I never asked and I don't remember her dating anyone in a while, and she did see her friend Michelle quite often.

Regardless, she was obviously happy with Shelley and that was all that mattered. I liked Shelley, both as a coach and a stepmom. It could have been weird, but it wasn't. Though they had been together since I had started high school, Shelley didn't live with us.

Once the competition was over, we spent the weekend in the city to enjoy the hotel, do some shopping, and indulge in fine dining. February's been so focused on the competition, I barely saw her speak to anyone all week. She found it hard to compete against her friends, so she tuned them out.

I guessed they all did it because she met up with her friends while she was in town. They spent the day at the mall, gossiping about the other teams, and pigging out on junk food. It's a rare treat.

They were on a strict diet and had basically been almost starving all week.

After brunch on Sunday, we headed home, and I spent the rest of the day and evening binge-watching TV shows. Mom even let me have dinner on a tray in the living room. I was still stuffed from lunch, but it was only baked chicken, steamed veggies, and plain yogurt. *Gotta get my protein!*

When the alarm went off at six the next days, I was dismayed to learn that February's routine was almost identical to January's where the vocal exercises were replaced by a round of ballet pliés at the bar installed in her room. Oh, and breakfast was a green protein smoothie. *Yuk!*

I checked my planner while I waited for the bus and realized that January and February had the exact same schedule with different teachers. When the lunch bell rang, I hopped on the bus that took us to our gymnastics club. Again, it was a thirty-minute ride and I ate on the bus. Lunch was bland but nutritious.

I chatted with the same friends from the weekend, Trish and Noemie. When we arrived, we split into levels and began the warm-up. Preparation, jump rope, head and wrist rolls, high toe walks, stretching, and splits. Then we spent some time working on each of the four skills.

When I got back to school, Mom was there to pick me up. Sweet! She handed me a sports drink and asked about my day. We chatted on the ten-minute ride home and she told me my dinner was in the oven. She had to work tonight and would be home by nine.

I headed straight for the hot tub. *We have a hot tub!* The warm water and bubbles took the kinks out of the day. When my fifteen minutes were up, I hopped into the shower and put on my pajamas.

I had a solitary dinner in the kitchen while reading a short story for English Language Arts class. After dinner, I got my homework done, brushed my teeth and I was in bed by nine. I was wiped.

The next morning, Mom asked if I minded walking to ballet class after school since she had to work. I told her it was fine. It's only a ten-minute walk from home and the fresh air would do me good.

At lunchtime, I was happy to report that February did not do her homework. Instead, she was registered in a half-hour yoga class that started right after the lunch bell. Trish and Noemie took it too. We had lunch on a bench outside after the class. We were very relaxed and didn't have much to say.

Ballet class was interesting. It's a multi-age group and it's not a competitive class. It's my understanding that the point was to work on flexibility and grace to improve the floor events. The Zumba class on Thursdays, after school, was to improve rhythm and coordination.

The week zipped by. On Friday night, Mom and I watched a movie together but by nine we were both in bed, exhausted. I think Mom worked a lot more in this reality. I assumed it's because gymnastics was an expensive sport. She never complained, and I was grateful for everything she did for me.

I spent Saturday morning at the club. We had a one-hour class called Mental Toughness Training. We worked on visualization, staying in the present, using a mantra, letting go of past failures, and the art of focusing. It's not bad.

Then came the tough part. We each had a strength training routine to follow. A few personal trainers were on hand to ensure we performed the exercises correctly so as not to cause injury. They were also very firm in their motivational speeches. Now I knew why we had a hot tub.

After a well-deserved soak and a huge lunch, I had a power nap. Now I was ready for homework, which I did straight until Mom called me for dinner.

To my surprise, Nana was here and she had brought dinner! I often ate with her on Saturdays because it was my high-carb day. Tonight, we were having spaghetti with meatballs, garlic bread, and apple pie a la mode. Shelley was also here to pick Mom up for date night.

This Nana was also planning a trip to Morocco. We spent the evening looking at pictures from her trip to Amsterdam and painting our toenails. She stayed over since Mom was staying at Shelley's.

On Sunday morning, we slept in, well until eight, and it felt like a splurge. Nana and I had breakfast and then she left to go to church. She made me a Mom-approved lunch in the fridge and told me Mom would be back for dinner.

I spent all day on homework, stopping only for lunch and a walk at midday. Mom and Shelley got back around four, soaked in the hot tub, and made dinner. We had dinner together and Shelley left after the dishes were done.

The next two and a half weeks were more of the same. On the twenty-sixth of March, six juniors and six seniors from the gym club piled into a bus with Shelley and two volunteer moms and headed for the first technical Elite competition in Ottawa. We would be there for two days, staying in hotel rooms, four girls to a room. I was staying with Trish, Noemie, and Sarah, Noemie's younger sister.

The vibe was a lot more intense than it had been at the competition in Montreal. This was a much bigger event and the stakes were higher. I would be a basket case, but February was calm, cool, and collected. Perhaps I should look into those Mental Toughness classes. They seemed to be paying off.

Thirty-two athletes got to compete at the Canadian Championships. Eight for each apparatus. There were two Technical trials. They retained the athlete's best score for each apparatus. If they were in the top eight in at least one event, and their total score was at least 18.6 out of 24, they were in. So, it was important to do well in all four events.

My performance on the bars was stellar and not only was I in the eight, but I was also in the top three. I couldn't believe I grabbed the last spot on the beam. Those ballet classes were a good idea. My total score was 18.8 and I was happy. I've got a month to keep working at it before the second trial.

The bus ride home was very quiet. We had been running on adrenaline and the team was wiped out. If January's life had made me feel like a slacker, February made me feel downright lazy, I thought before I fell asleep.

CHAPTER FOURTEEN

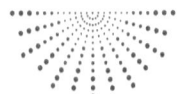

WHEN I OPENED MY EYES, APRIL WAS SITTING BESIDE ME. I STRETCHED, expecting to be sore from the last two days of competition, but I felt like I had just woken from a luxurious nap. I turned around, hoping to say a few words to February, but she was gone. So was the Teacher and all the other girls.

It was just January, April, and me on the sofa. I looked to January. Did she do this every night? Didn't she have better things to dream about than overseeing me swim through time and space?

"What exactly does being a team leader entail?" I asked her. She seemed to understand I needed this little palate cleanser before jumping into April's life.

"A team leader is, of course, responsible for the group and acts as their representative in larger gatherings," she said. Seeing the confusion on my face, she continued, "there are monthly meetings for each age group with one of the Managers. They keep tabs on what's going on in our lives and replace girls as needed."

"You mean like if a girl's timeline changes drastically, she moves to another group, right?"

"Yes. And with every birthday, the groups are reassessed based on reality similarities. Under the age of sixteen, there is a lot of movement due to the parents' decisions. The older we get, the more stable our groups tend to be. Girls also need to be replaced when they die," she replied.

I made an 'o' with my mouth and nodded. Right, we all died. But the moment we died was different based on the reality we were in. Before I started wondering how I might die, I pushed the thought away and asked, "is that it? Any special privileges?"

January smiled. "As Team Leader, I get to be January. This means I have access to all the memories of the last year instead of only the last month. It saves us from having to interact with too many girls when we want to change something. The position is also a pre-requisite to becoming a Teacher, which is my goal," said January.

"Oh, cool," I said, and I could feel April getting antsy beside me. Accessing the timeline was all that stood between her and what she wanted to do. Though I'd still have May through December to visit, she'd be good to go. Well, she still needed our agreement. Which I assume we'd provide in some kind of group meeting.

I smiled at her and held out my hands. Though I was not all that keen on visiting her life, I couldn't wait to see Dad again.

* * *

I BRACED MYSELF FOR SOME KIND OF DEBATE CLUB CAMP, BUT WHEN I opened my eyes I saw I was drooling on Penny's shoulder. She's asleep too, her head resting on the plane's window. A peek outside revealed turquoise blue ocean for miles. A rush of excitement came over me. I turned to tell Mom to look, but I came face to face with Dad. He was looking at me in amusement.

"Can't beat the view, right?" he said, then turned to nudge Mom. She was asleep in the seat across the aisle. When she didn't wake up, he gave up and turned back to me. "Bob told me they have free snorkeling trips every day. Can you imagine looking at tropical fish in that water?" he asked.

"I can't wait! When do we land?" I asked.

Dad checked the wall monitor and told me we would land in about thirty minutes. As though on cue, the captain came on the air and told us we'd be landing shortly and that the flight attendant would be going down the aisles to pick up the trash.

Dad kissed my forehead and got up to go back to his seat next to Mom. Penny woke up and whooped when she looked out the window. I'd want to pretend it was no big deal, but April was a good sister and they squealed together. *Cozumel, here we come!*

Once we had landed, gone through customs, and picked up our luggage, we headed for the row of buses taking guests to the all-inclusive resorts. I kept an eye out for the Royal Cozumel Resort and spotted it, four buses from the last.

Penny and I could no longer contain ourselves, and ran all the way to the bus. It was too nice out to get on the bus, so we waited for Mom and Dad to catch up. Besides, Mom had our travel papers.

It was a short bus ride to the hotel and the view was amazing all the way. We were greeted with mocktails and loud fiesta music. This was going to be so much fun. I was literally as excited as April was. It's the first family vacation we've had to take a plane for.

We usually spent March break at home since my parents had to work. Our annual trip happened in July. Nana's friend had a cottage in Prince Edward Island that she rented to us for two weeks every year. It was amazing, but this was going to be *epic*.

For one thing, the water would be clear and warm. Even in late July, the water in PEI never went above twenty degrees Celsius. In Cozumel, the daily average was twenty-six degrees. Also, the sand here was fine and white, whereas it was blown and grainy over there. Oh, and did I mention they had six pools, a club just for teens, and a seaside mini-waterpark?

On the ride up the elevator, we checked out our bracelets. They're purple and let us eat and drink anything, anywhere, anytime on the resort. Non-alcoholic, of course. Mom and Dad's bracelets were blue.

On the eleventh floor, the bellboy led the way and opened the door to our suite. A suite! While Dad was tipping him, I already had my phone out, taking a thousand pictures, and Penny and I scrambled to the deck just off the living room.

Beach and ocean. For miles. I took a deep breath and inhaled the salty air. I was grinning ear to ear when I felt Dad's hand on my shoulders. In a rush of love, I turned and hugged him really tight. "Thank you, thank you, thank you!" I said, my voice muffled in his shirt.

"You're welcome, starfish. I hope you girls have fun. Have you checked out your room?" he asked, pointing to the right. I realized just then that there were, in fact, three balconies. The one on the right had a divider.

Penny and I looked at each other and rushed back into the living room. The door to our bedroom was open and Dad had placed our luggage on the luggage stands at the end of the beds. He knew us well. Penny had the one near the wall. I had the bed nearest the window.

I was torn between throwing the patio doors open, jumping on the bed like Penny was doing, or snapping pics before she messed up the whole room.

I opted for taking photos. We had our own outer door and bathroom. We even had a fridge, a coffeemaker, and some snacks. The bed was comfy, and the view on the deck was the same as on the other deck.

I posted the pics to my account and shot off a quick message to Sam and Julie. Heading back to the living room, I followed Mom's and Dad's voices to their room. It's similar to ours in decor but it's a lot bigger. They had an ensuite bathroom, but no door leading out of the room. They had a small seating area in front of the patio doors, and their patio had lounge chairs in addition to the regular chairs and table.

"Put your suits on and let's meet in the kitchen in ten minutes," he said, and we made off like fiends.

Back in the kitchen, Dad laid out the map of the resort. He told us there was also an interactive app we could download. He pointed out the area where the cabana he and Mom had rented for the week was. He wanted us to meet there twice a day to make sure everyone was alright. He expected us to have dinner together every night at eight in the evening. Otherwise, Penny and I were free.

Mom said I could only leave Penny if she was at the kids' club under adult supervision and I should keep my phone on me at all times, with the location tracker on. Dad had given us these waterproof cases to keep our phones in and there was a chip in our bracelets so we didn't need door keys.

"Should we go down for lunch?" I asked tentatively.

"Your mom and I want to unpack and have a drink here on the deck first. You know, to settle in. But you guys can go on ahead. We should be at the cabana by two in the evening. And we'll have our phones too," he replied. Penny was pulling my arm towards the door.

"Go on, get the lay of the land," said Mom and I gave in to Penny.

I suggested we grab lunch and do a quick recon mission, then come back for our stuff for the beach. Penny was nodding, but I could tell she was not listening. I laughed and we waved goodbye to Mom and Dad.

On the way down, I installed the app on my phone. I checked the time and told Penny we had three options for lunch. Her eyes bugged out when I mentioned the *all-day-burgers-and-fries* restaurant. Ok, off to *The Grill*.

It proved to be a great choice. *The Grill* was on the oceanfront, didn't require a shirt—only shoes—and also had tacos, chips, and a DIY ice cream swirl machine with loads of topping choices. Penny's in Heaven, and I admit this was the sweet life. We grabbed a table overlooking the ocean and the waiter brought us a couple of iced teas.

After lunch, we headed to the beach to check out the water temperature. It was heavenly, and I had to peel Penny back to keep her from heading in. I told her we needed to let lunch sink in a bit before we went swimming.

First up on our tour was the kids' club. There were actually three clubs. The baby club, which was basically daycare. Then, the kids' club that was for kids six to twelve. It was a lot like day camp. Some kids were registered for the week. They reported every morning after breakfast and parents picked them up again at four. Penny could come and go as she pleased. It was a family vacation, and our parents wanted to spend time with us.

Next was the teen club, for kids thirteen to eighteen. The legal drinking age in Cozumel was the same as in Canada, eighteen. The club was actually the teen bar. Most of the activities were up on the board. They didn't start until noon and ran until ten at night.

We went to check out the pools and grabbed our complimentary beach towels while we were there. Mom and Dad would have to get their own because it was one towel per bracelet per day.

When we got to the room, my parents were just about ready to head out. They waited for Penny and me to gather our stuff and we all went down together.

The week was amazing. It had been a while since April had so much fun with her family. I, on the other hand, had never felt this innate sense of belonging. I was tan, happy, and couldn't wait to see Sam by the time we were on the plane trip back.

CHAPTER FIFTEEN

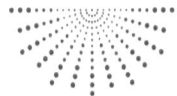

OUR PERFECT FAMILY VACATION WAS COMPLETELY RUINED MINUTES before we reached the elevator to the parking garage. When Dad handed in our declaration and passports at the last checkpoint, he was swiftly escorted through a door simply labelled "Authorized Personnel Only." It happened so fast that he was gone before we even knew what happened.

Meanwhile, Mom, Penny, and I were ushered into a nearby room. Mom tried to get information out of the female customs officer, but all she told us was to stay put and await further instructions.

I had seen enough movies to recognize it as an interrogation room. I tried the door and when I found it locked, I started to panic. "Mom, they've locked us in!" I shrieked.

"Don't be ridiculous," replied Mom, as she tried the handle. Color drained from her face and she knocked on the door. "Excuse me? Can someone open the door? We've been locked in," she said in a strained voice. There was no response from the other side.

I did the same, but on what I assume was a double-sided mirror on the wall. Nothing.

Penny looked up from her tablet and asked, "where's Dad? Did he go and get the car?"

I looked to Mom. She looked at me, then at Penny. "Yes, dear. He'll be back in a little while." Penny put her headphones back on and resumed her game. She moved closer to me and said in a low voice, "I don't know what's going on, but we should avoid talking in here until we know what's going on."

I took Penny to sit on some chairs. I grabbed my phone and checked my messages.

Mom made a call. "Riley, it's me. I need your help. I know this isn't your area of expertise, but we're being detained by the authorities at the Montreal airport. I'm alone in a room with the kids, and they've taken Parker somewhere else," she said.

Mom answered a few of Uncle Riley's questions. I guessed he was a lawyer in this reality, too. After a minute or two, she thanked him and hung up. She checked her watch and frowned. She seemed to be debating with herself.

She made another call. "Hi Mom. I don't want you to worry. We're still at the airport waiting on some misplaced luggage. We'll probably grab dinner on the way home and get in later than planned. Is it okay if I call you tomorrow?" she asked. Nana had apparently agreed as Mom ended the call with a happy, "thanks, love you!"

Now I knew Mom was worried. She never lied to Nana. She came over to where we were and asked, "are you kids hungry? I've got some protein bars in my purse." I shook my head and kept scrolling. Mom waved a peanut butter bar in front of Penny. She grabbed it and started eating.

Mom peered at my phone and said, "it might be best if we keep this to ourselves for now."

"I figured as much. I told Sam the same story you told Nana and told him I'd see him tomorrow. It's a ped day, anyway," I replied, acting way calmer than I felt.

April clearly had better emotional control than I did. I'd still be knocking on the door to be let out. After she texted Sam and Julie, she started searching the internet for reasons why people might be detained at the airport.

Mom's phone rang and we both jumped. "Riley? What's going on?"

she asked a little shrilly. She got up and moved away from me, presumably so I couldn't hear what she had to say.

Her hand flew to her mouth and she exclaimed, *"what?"* This was bad. I was still hoping this was a random inspection. According to the internet, it happened. Mom was shaking her head in disbelief and thanking Riley for his help.

There's no time to ask her what's going on as the door opened and two uniformed officers came in, one of which was the officer that brought us here, along with a lady in a power suit.

She headed straight for Mom and put out her hand. "Hello, Mrs. Knox. I'm Isabelle Lariviere. I'm an attorney at Tremblay and Smith. My colleague, Michel Beaumont, is currently with your husband." Mom shook the woman's hand, bewildered, and looked at the officers waiting by the door. One of them had a slightly different uniform and she looked like a regular cop.

"The Canadian Border Agency has detained your family on behalf of the Sureté du Québec. Your husband and his attorney have been escorted to the downtown precinct for questioning. You and the children are free to go," she said.

When Mom was about to talk, she shook her head just a little and added, "your husband has given me the keys to your car and parking voucher." She placed the items in Mom's hand. "Are you okay to drive?" she asked. "If not, I can drive you home, and this uniformed officer will follow us and drive me back."

Mom snapped to attention. "No, I'm fine. Just surprised and confused," she said, pocketing the keys and voucher. "Clare, get your sister, we're going home."

Once we gathered our luggage, the officer opened the door and let us out of the room. We followed the attorney up to the parking garage level. It was cold and we all donned our winter parkas before heading to the car. No one said a word as we made our way to the car, loaded the bags in the trunk, and got inside.

She handed Mom her card and said, "call me when you get home."

CHAPTER SIXTEEN

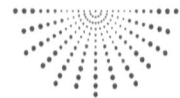

As Mom pulled out of the garage, Penny looked up from her game and yelled, "hey, aren't we waiting for Dad?"

"Sorry, shrimp," I said ruffling her hair. "Dad had to work. He'll meet us back home later." Her eyes narrowed at me. As oblivious as she had been until now, she could tell this is a bunch of baloney.

"The police had questions for Dad. I don't know what they want to know or how long he'll be there," said Mom, resigned. She stopped at the first drive-through she saw and we ordered some food. It should keep us busy on the hour-long drive home.

Mom put on the radio and focused on the road. When Penny went to ask her something else, I put my hand on her mouth and told her Mom needed to concentrate on the road. She rifled through her backpack and found the candy we bought at the airport.

Happy, she munched on it and watched a movie on her tablet. Taking my cue from her, I pulled up some of the shows I downloaded for the trip and never got around to watch.

When we got home, Mom asked us to unpack, put our dirty laundry in the hamper, and put away our suitcases. She locked herself in her room, presumably to call the lawyer. She didn't come out for over an hour.

When she did, I could see she'd been crying. She told us it's time for bed. It was eight-thirty, which was Penny's bedtime and not mine, but I didn't argue. As we said good night to Penny, Mom pulled out her phone and dialled Dad's number. She held it out to Penny.

I didn't know what he told her, but Penny smiled, told Dad goodnight, and gave the phone to me as she snuggled in for the night. Mom kissed her forehead and we left her room.

"Dad? What's going on?" I asked, tears blinding me as I made for my room. Mom didn't follow.

"Hey, Clare. I'm sorry about all that. It's just a misunderstanding. It seems some money is missing in some of our accounts and they are trying to figure it all out. I had to answer some questions," he said casually.

"But did they need to pick you up at the airport? Why not just ask you to come in tomorrow when you go back to work?" I asked him, smelling a rat.

"It's really complicated. They've closed the office and wanted to catch me before I went in or had a chance to talk to the other bankers. Because we were away this week, they were waiting on my input. Sweetie, don't worry. It's going to be okay. The officers were just doing their jobs. I'm not in jail or anything. In fact, I'm at the downtown flat. I'm too tired to come home. I'll get an Uber and see you tomorrow," he promised.

It sounded reasonable, and if I planned to get any sleep tonight, I had to believe him. "Ok, Dad. Be safe. I love you," I said in a strangled voice.

"Sleep tight, Clarabelle," he said before hanging up. He hadn't called me that in a while. I would normally roll my eyes, but tonight I found it oddly comforting. I came out of my room and hugged mom. She was standing just outside the doorway.

I could see she didn't want to talk about it. I got it, we both needed our beauty sleep. I handed her the phone and said goodnight.

* * *

DAD CAME HOME THE NEXT DAY AFTER LUNCH. HE AND MOM THOUGHT they had been clever keeping Penny and me in the dark, but early this morning, I was scrolling through the news. I found some headlines from last week about the fraud charges at Dad's bank.

They detained and questioned everyone from the CEO to the night watchman. Four corporate bankers were arrested on Friday. This morning, they arrested a fifth and released their names to the press. Parker Knox was among them.

I waited for him to unpack, shower, and change into jeans and a t-shirt. When he finally assembled us in the dining room for a family meeting, I couldn't help being angry. I wish I had a proper newspaper to slap in front of him. It would be more dramatic.

Instead, I shoved my phone under his nose and cocked my head. "Explain." Mom frowned at me and was about to tell me to watch my tone and respect my elders or some such crap. I knew that look.

But Dad only sighed and hung his head. *Oh, God!* I thought. *He's guilty.* I pulled the phone back and put it in my pocket. Mom started crying and Penny had the look she got when she was wondering what she was in trouble for. She started to fidget.

There's a knock at the door, and Nana's head popped in as she let herself in. Dad shot Mom an accusing look. Mom ignored him and rushed to her own mother. Nana held Mom for a bit, stroking her hair and back. I could hear her saying "it's going to be alright." She gave Mom a piece of tissue she pulled from her pocket.

Stepping out of her boots, she dropped her coat on the back of one of the dining room chairs. She kissed my temple and went to sit with Penny, who was too old to be sitting on her lap, but no one mentioned it.

"Good morning, Parker. I hear you had a rough night and the morning hasn't been all that great either," she told him.

Mom sat next to him and he took her hand for support. Mom was clearly upset with him, but she let him. He nodded at Nana's statement and took a deep breath.

"Guys, I messed up," he started. "Big time. Here's the truth. One of our clients offered a few of us the chance to invest in a new venture.

This guy had the Midas touch, everything he touched turned to gold. It was a great opportunity. But none of us had enough capital, so we decided to borrow it from some clients, fully intending to pay it back with dividends once the venture was up and running."

"These clients you were borrowing from, did they give you their consent?" Nana asked. Her face was neutral, she was gathering information before she made any hasty judgements. I decided to do the same.

"Not in so many words. However, we *are* legally allowed to move funds between accounts on a short-term basis," he hedged.

"Yes, of course. However, I don't think your personal account is among those you can transfer to," said Nana shrewdly. She had a point.

"That's true. But we created an account in trust for all of us. The money never even left the bank, nor did it ever enter our personal accounts. The accounts we drew on would have benefited greatly from the investment, if we'd had time to implement it," he said at last.

"Ok, so it wasn't illegal, but it wasn't right. And you were caught before you could put the money back, which made it illegal," I said, checking that I was understanding this right.

"Yes, that's basically what happened," he acknowledged.

"So, what happens now?" I asked.

"I was arrested last night and spent the night in jail. This morning, I went before the judge and was released until the trial. Don't freak out, there won't be a trial. Not for me anyway. The attorney suggested I accept the settlement drafted by the prosecuting attorney," he explained.

"And what are the terms of the settlement?" asked Nana. Mom started to cry again. She already knew.

"I plead guilty to the charge in exchange for a reduced sentence," he said.

"You're going to jail?" I screamed, standing up abruptly. Nana rubbed my back and urged me to sit back down again.

"I'd be sent to the minimum-security unit in Sorel for nine months. If I went to trial and was found guilty, I would get a minimum of two years up to a maximum of fourteen years because the overall sum was over one million dollars. But since we never actually took the money out of the bank, we've been offered a conditional sentence," he said.

"What about your job?" I asked. "And why can't you go to the Cowansville jail?"

"I could never work in a bank again. And likely not for any government agency because I'll have been convicted of a criminal offence," he answered, rubbing his face with his hands. "As for the jail, only those with a sentence over two years go to a federal penitentiary. And besides, the Cowansville prison is a medium-security facility."

Penny had been listening attentively. "So basically, Daddy did a bad thing and now he's being punished," she said matter-of-factly.

"That sounds about right, kiddo," he replied.

She hopped off Nana's lap and went to him. Earnestly, she placed her hands on either side of his face and asked, "do you promise never to do it again?"

Dad nodded, tears in his eyes. "I promise," he said gruffly.

Penny kissed his forehead and asked, "can we visit you in jail?"

Dad hung his head and replied, "there are visiting hours every day, honey. Mom will decide when the best time to visit might be."

She thought about this for a minute and finally said, "so it's like camp. When do you leave? When would you come home?"

"If I accept the settlement, I'll have another hearing later this week and would likely be expected at the penitentiary this weekend. I would likely be home by Christmas," he said.

Penny said a quick "ok" and left the room to go watch cartoons on TV.

"But you're going to take the deal, right?" I asked.

"I don't see that I have a better option," he replied.

CHAPTER SEVENTEEN

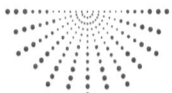

THE NEXT DAY, PENNY AND I WENT BACK TO SCHOOL. I HAD PETITIONED my parents to stay home with Dad this week, seeing as he would be going away for a long time, but they didn't go for it. Then I tried again on the grounds that everyone at school would know about Dad's arrest and it would be awkward and humiliating.

Mom called the principal however and was assured there would be no bullying or awkwardness. They had a team that dealt with this kind of situation. Should things go south, the principal would send me home.

Last night, I texted Sam and Julie and they walked me to my first-period class. But when I got there, a counsellor was waiting for me outside the door. Sam kissed me and said he'd be back after his math class and Julie squeezed my arm and went into the classroom to take her seat.

While I was having a chat in the counsellor's office, a member of the staff was talking to the rest of the group, providing minimal information, and ways to support me in this trying time. Julie later said it was a nice speech and most students responded with compassion to my situation.

By lunch, word had spread and though I did get a few more stares than usual, most were accompanied with smiles of understanding. It was too cold to eat outside yet, so we requested permission to eat in the debate team's room. Mrs. Newman, our debate coach, was there, but she stayed in her tiny office grading papers.

"How do you feel?" asked Julie, patting my hand.

"I'm angry at my dad for doing this. It makes me want to become a lawyer even more. It's just so easy to get away with white-collar crime," I replied. So far, I had been so caught up in April's life that I hadn't had a chance to process how *I* would feel in the situation. I didn't think I would be angry. I'd be disappointed in my dad, scared about him going to jail, and worried about the impact on our family. It's hard to know how I'd feel if I'd had my dad around all these years. Maybe I would take him for granted.

After lunch, we went to our respective classes and met up again after school. The day went smoothly as did the rest of the week.

Meanwhile, Dad got his affairs in order and on Friday night we drove him to the detention centre. He showed us pictures from the website, and it didn't seem so bad. It actually looked nicer than our high school. I recognized the visitors' waiting and visiting rooms from the vision April had shared with me from further ahead.

We were told that every two months, with good behaviour, inmates could invite their family to visit for up to three days. There were little 'cottages' set up on the grounds with two bedrooms, a kitchen, a living room, and a private bathroom. There was also a playground and a basketball court for what was termed *Private Family Visits* (PFV).

The officer told us we'd receive a list of instructions if and when the time came. Grandparents were also welcome, but Dad's parents had died a long time ago and I couldn't imagine Nana being interested in such a thing.

An adult was required for a PFV, but not for the weekly visits. This was why I was able to visit with Sam. He had repeated a year in elementary school, so he already had his licence.

In addition to weekly in-person visits, Dad could apply for video visits. He could use his internet privileges to have a videoconference with members of his immediate family. They had to be set-up forty-eight hours in advance and could last no longer than fifty minutes.

We agreed on a schedule that Dad could submit for approval. It was better than I had anticipated. We'd still have access to Dad regularly.

When we entered the detention facility, it became all too real. The building was new, everything was spotless yet purposefully matte. Other than the reinforced glass, there were no reflective surfaces. As though anything shinny would spark a rebellion. Or perhaps it was an additional way of scrubbing out the inmate's law-breaking identity.

The waiting room was empty. The guard behind the glass, and likely those watching the camera feeds, was the only witness to our family drama.

"Okay, guys. This is the end of the line," said dad, opening his arms, inviting one of us to embrace him. Penny rushes at him, all smiles. For her, this is an adventure. One she will likely milk for all it's worth at school next week.

"Have fun, daddy. I hope you make new friends while you're here," she says, and we can't help but laugh. It relieves some of the tension but not the cold that has seeped into my bones.

It's like a crew of dementors had swept the place just before we arrived and were still lurking, eager to suck the joy out of the room for the next arrival.

Mom went next. They'd been fighting all week. Mom was angry that he had put her in the position of having to deal with us, the house, and the bills all by herself. It looked like they may have made up in the last twenty-four hours. Or perhaps she had realized she should let go of her anger and show a little more compassion for what dad was going through. Either way, they embraced warmly and kissed like they may never see each other again. If they hadn't been my parents, it would have been romantic. As it was, it was just awkward.

It was my turn. Mom took Penny to sit in the waiting area, giving dad and me a little privacy. Though I was very disappointed in him, I was still daddy's little girl. The look in dad's eyes made me think we thought he'd lost her.

I let him wrap his arms around me, savouring the extra tight hug April was giving him. It was one of those moments where time seems to stand still. I was acutely aware of the feel of his shirt against my skin, and the love that poured out of him, warming me to my core.

Dad had shaved and the smell of his aftershave would linger with me long after I'd returned to my own reality. As would the featherlight kiss he placed on my head.

"I promise I'll do better," he said, his voice cracking with emotion. I hugged him tighter still and replied, "I know you will."

On the drive home, everyone was quiet. The reality of seeing Dad at the prison, though not behind bars, had stunned us into silent reflections. Even Penny was staring out the window, her tablet forgotten on her lap.

Over the weekend, Nana came over and livened things up. It was too early to visit Dad, he had to get settled, get to know the other inmates, find a job, and meet with his counsellor. Nana tried to get me to go out with my friends, but all I wanted was to curl up in a ball and wait for Dad to come home.

On Monday, Mom insisted that I go to school. I felt better once I was there, and life started to make sense again. The next two weeks dragged on and I was looking forward to getting out of this reality.

On Wednesdays, I had a somewhat private chat with Dad for twenty minutes. Mom had to be visible in the shot, so she sat reading the paper at the dining room table and I angled my laptop so my back was to her and she could be seen through my bedroom door.

Penny had her twenty minutes when I was done while Mom sat next to her and pretended not to be paying attention. It worked. It was like Dad was at an out-of-town conference.

On Saturdays, we drove over to visit him and spent a couple of hours there. When the weather was warmer, we could have the visits in a special courtyard. But for now, it was in the visitors' room.

When the last day of March finally arrived, I was more than ready to go back to the yellow room. Before bed, I hugged Penny and drank in her features. Spending time with her and Dad had been a treat, and I got why April wanted to go back in time and try to change things. If she could convince Dad not to do it, her life was going to be awesome.

CHAPTER EIGHTEEN

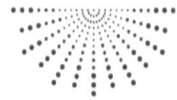

WHEN I OPENED MY EYES AND SAW APRIL SITTING NEXT TO ME, I wrapped my arms around her and said, "I'm so sorry that happened to you!"

She nodded sadly and got up to leave. "I'll let you get on with your visits. We'll talk soon," she said and faded out of sight.

"Hey, I'm May," said a girl from behind me. I twisted back to look at her, but she had already taken April's seat.

"Hi, I'm March," I replied lamely. She smiled. She and I were wearing the same outfit; blue fleece pyjama bottoms and a black top with the words 'Fabulous' written in rainbow letters.

"Do you need a break?" she asked.

"That depends on what I'm about to walk into," I said warily. I was not actually tired. I wondered if all this activity would upset my sleep cycle. *Do I even have time to dream regular dreams when I'm here?* I wondered.

She had that secret smile I had when I was trying not to spill the beans. "Let's just say you'll feel right at home in my life," she replied cryptically.

I turned my palms face up and she slapped them like she was playing pattycake.

* * *

AT FIRST, I THOUGHT THERE HAD BEEN A MISTAKE AND I HAD WOKEN UP at home in *my* reality. Same pyjamas, same room, same house. Mom was in the kitchen making coffee. She was in her pyjamas too.

On the last three visits, I had arrived on Sunday night before March break begun. I was confused. May gave Mom a hug and took a sip from her coffee.

"Make your own!" she exclaimed.

"I only need a sip. If I take any more, I'll get addicted. Like you," I replied sweetly.

Mom shook her head at me and asked what I had planned for the day.

"I'm meeting Mel, Julie, and Sam at the lake after lunch," I said, putting bread in the toaster.

"Make sure you keep your distance," she replied from her desk.

May replied, "don't worry, Mom. We'll be safe." Mom put her headphones on and started working. Was she working on a Sunday?

May poured orange juice in a glass and took a sip while she waited for the toasts to pop out and I was left wondering about what Mom had said about distance. Was she worried I'd fall through the ice? The lake's been frozen solid for over a month. We always checked the city website before heading out. I shook my head. *Moms are weird.*

After breakfast, May settled on the couch to read *The Giver*. By the time I would have visited each of my other realities, there was a chance that it no longer would be one of my favourite books. For now, I read along.

Right before lunch, Mom told me she's going for a walk and asked if I wanted to join her. I declined, saying I would get enough fresh air and exercise when I went skating. It was a short walk and when she came back, I had warmed up some chilli for us to eat.

Mom couldn't give me a ride, she had to work. It turned out to be Monday. I walked the two and a half kilometres to the lake, cutting through the woods. What a difference six weeks made, I thought. When I walked this path a few days ago, it was mid-April and full-on spring. Now, the path was iced over, it was below freezing, and I was happy I had put on my long johns under my jeans.

I was the last to arrive at the lake. The others were seated on outdoor benches putting their skates on. It was so weird, they were sitting really far apart. I was actually wondering why they were not inside where it was warm.

May headed to an empty bench and started putting on her skates. I passed an elderly couple on my way and saw they were wearing surgical masks. I frowned, but May just kept walking. Once we all had our skates on, we took turns going down the ramp to the lake, so as not to bump into each other. Why would that matter? Wasn't that half the fun, bumping into each other and falling on our butts?

On the lake, all the adults were wearing masks like the elderly people. Only children and teenagers didn't have them. This was very odd—to me anyway. No one else seemed bothered by it and my friends didn't comment on it.

We skated in a square formation, two meters apart. The two in front were skating backwards so we could talk and we switched places after a while. Now I knew something was wrong. It was like we were all in that movie, *Six Feet Apart*.

I was trying to figure it out. Some people were close, holding hands even, while others were like us, keeping their distance. I guess they're couples. The families were close too. This was so weird.

After about an hour, we're all frozen and decided to head back to put our freezing boots on. I was dying for a hot chocolate from the vendor inside, but there was a sign on the door saying that they were closed due to COVID-19. What the heck was that? Was there an outbreak of some kind? Was that why a lot of people were wearing masks?

It's so frustrating being a passenger in this life! I wanted answers and I couldn't get online and look it up. I would just have to wait and see, which was not my strong suit!

There were no hugs goodbye, only air kisses and a promise to meet up online later to play a game called 'Among Us.' I made the trek home, jumped in the shower to warm up, and then made myself a hot chocolate.

Now that I thought about it, why was Mom working in her pyjamas? Though she mostly worked from home, she still put on her work clothes and a pair of earrings every day. Probably had something to do with that COVID-19 thing.

I grabbed my laptop and headed for the living room in case our game got rowdy and disturbed Mom. We had a great time and all too soon Mom was telling me to come help with dinner.

Other than having to wear masks and sit apart at the movies, March break turned out to be pretty much the same as the one I had. When school started up again, that's where the biggest differences set in.

First, Mom worked from home a hundred percent of the time now. Any interviews she needed to conduct were done through videoconference. This wouldn't be an issue, except school was also online.

Mom and I had to coordinate our schedules so we could talk freely while not disturbing the other. We set up a rolling workstation either of us could move to another room for added privacy.

I really enjoyed remote school but May missed seeing her friends every day. It occurred to me that we didn't see Nana as much, and only outside our respective homes. Since Nana hated the cold, she mostly dropped by and stayed in her car while Mom and I froze and talked through the window.

I learned that this had been going on for about a year and folks were optimistic. They had just rolled out a vaccine and life would probably go back to being normal-ish within the year.

I took two walks every day to stay sane and compensate for the lack of Phys. Ed. classes and sitting on my butt all day. Mom did the same, but we didn't go at the same time. We spent enough time together as it was and this was the only alone time we got.

Most of my friends complained about spending so much time with their families. The news reported an all-time high of domestic abuse cases as well as mental health issues, in addition to the daily mortality rate due to the virus.

But things at home were great. Mom and I had actually grown closer from spending so much time together. She was checking that I was ok, worried I might feel isolated.

She hardly left the house other than for exercise. She had our groceries delivered, shopped online, and didn't see her friends. I was growing worried about *her*. But she said she liked it better this way, and that her friends understood.

I, on the other hand, saw my friends as often as the weather permitted. The warmer it got, the happier we were. We mostly went sledding or skating, but soon we would be walking when the iced melted. And we played games or chatted online, which we used to do anyway.

They said we humans could adapt to anything, and it had to be true. Otherwise, why would May stick it out if she didn't have to? Technically, she could jump right into my life and put this whole pandemic behind her.

Now I was wondering if the other girls even knew about my life. May had intimated that she knew it looked a lot like hers. Did my whole year load into their memories when I started coming to Clarity Castle? I'd have to ask the Teacher or January.

Maybe I needed to get through all the March memories as well for any of us to be able to make significant changes, not just April.

At the end of the month, I was a little sad to be leaving. I was very comfortable in May's life and wondered if it was worth exploring a switch. I know it sounded crazy but it was a cozy life. Why would anyone willingly jump into a timeline where there was an outbreak of a killer virus?

CHAPTER NINETEEN

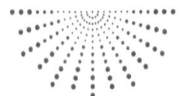

I woke up in my own bed. Had I gotten the dates wrong? Checking my phone, I saw that it was indeed the seventeenth of April. Why hadn't I gone back to the Castle? Maybe they hadn't meant for me to visit all of the realities in one go.

I was relieved. I felt like I had been gone for months when I had merely been asleep for ten hours. It boggled the mind.

I got up and saw Mom at her computer, headphones off. She was on Facebook. When she heard me, she got up to give me a hug. I held her just a little longer than usual.

"Are you feeling okay?" she asked as she checked my forehead.

I kissed her cheeks and replied, "I had a nightmare last night. Now that I see it was only a dream, I feel fantastic!"

Which I realized was true. I berated myself for even entertaining the thought of choosing May's reality. Okay, I was not thrilled about my upcoming Phys. Ed classes. The French classes, however, were actually worse when done online. There was so much more talking required!

And if I wanted Mom and me to be closer, I could just intend it the way I had intended a better grade on my exam. For that matter, I could totally change my perspective about gym class. If February was any indication, I had some badass genes in me somewhere. I could activate them and enhance my physical performance. Or take a page from January's playbook and increase my general confidence. *Yes, that's what I'd do.*

After breakfast, I went to my room to do my homework. At around ten, I got a text from Sam.

"Do you need help going over the math concepts before the test?" he wrote.

I lied and replied, *"no, I'm good. Thanks for offering!"* and added a "hug" emoji for good measure.

His response came quickly, *"you bet. TTL!"*

The truth was, I was still weirded out by the memories of him as my boyfriend. How would I ever look him in the eye again? I tried to imagine Sam as anything but my best friend and I couldn't. It gave me the creeps.

My concentration was shot and I checked the time. It was a little too early for lunch, so I decided to go for a walk. The weather was gorgeous and I was glad I had come out. I walked to the woods and headed for the quarry. No castle.

I headed to the lake, but I didn't sit to bask in the sun. I was afraid I'd pop right back to the Castle, and I would prefer to enjoy *this* moment. The weather had been unseasonably warm and a lot of people had come out to enjoy the trails. I didn't want to risk zoning out and having people think there was something wrong with me. Hopefully, it was only a temporary glitch that I lately appeared at the Castle every time I relaxed. Otherwise, I'd never be relaxed again!

Now that I knew I could choose to go anytime, and could for sure go every night, I assumed there was really no need to seize every opportunity.

When I got home, Mom had made burgers on the grill. She was getting Spring fever too!

"Do you want to eat outside?" she asked.

I would normally decline on account of killer hornets and the like. But as they had likely not gotten the memo that spring had arrived early, I figured we'd be safe.

"Sure," I said while wondering how we would manage it without a table and chairs. As though reading my mind, mom said, "I'll need your help getting the patio set out of the garage. For now, I think we can balance our plates on our laps and sit in the chairs around the firepit."

We had lunch and chatted about when we'd open the pool for the summer. Mom liked to do it early in the season because she said the water didn't need so many chemicals and, with the solar cover, the water would be ready when we were.

I got a few more hours of homework done before Mom reminded me about the patio set. It took us no more than fifteen minutes, but now that I was out, I didn't want to go back in. I texted Mel and asked if she wanted to go for a bike ride. She replied with three side laugh-out-loud emojis.

I replied with a bicycle emoji and prayer hands.

"We haven't gone for a bike ride in ages. Why not? Let me just make sure I still have a bike and get back to you," she texted back.

I had to make sure as well, I realized. I went back into the garage and added air to my tires. I brought the bike out near the front of the house. Mom was putting away the shovels.

"Are you *sure* you're feeling alright?" she said when she saw the bike.

Just then, Mel texted back and said she'd meet me at the lake in five minutes. *Yes!*

"What? It's Springtime and we've been cooped up inside all winter," I said in my defence.

Mom shrugged but reminded me I needed to wear a helmet. *Ugh.* I rode back to the garage, wiped the cobwebs from my helmet, and put it on. As I rode to the lake, I wondered why I stopped riding my bike. This was so much fun, a lot faster than walking. Okay, the helmet felt goofy, but I noticed I wasn't the only one wearing one. Even Mel had one on when I got to the lake.

We rode around town until it was time to go home for dinner. Now that I could intend good grades, it seemed I'd have more time for fun and friends. We agreed to do it again tomorrow and to invite Julie and Sam too. I'd just have to push the memories of Sam and me as a couple at the back of my brain.

As I rode home, I was fantasizing that Nana would be there with lasagna, garlic bread, and apple pie until I remembered she had left for her trip to Morocco. When I got home, however, Mom had ordered our favourite Hawaiian pizza and she had made brownies for dessert!

After washing my hands, I asked if she wanted me to get the salad going and she replied, "let's skip it, tonight." She looked at my astonished face and added, "and how about we eat in front of the TV while we watch our movie?"

I was slack-jawed. No veggies and eating in front of the TV had to be among the restricted activities in every parent's manual. Since it was not my birthday, I couldn't imagine what had gotten into her. Before I even knew how to respond, I was saying, "I love you, Mom," and rushing into her arms.

She laughed and pulled me in closer. "If I had known that's all it took, I'd have stunted your growth and done this years ago," she joked.

Aware that this display of affection was not entirely due to the meal, I was having a hard time expressing how much I appreciated the mom I had in this reality, and could only imagine how that would go over were I to say it out loud. Instead, I said, "that's not it. I just don't tell you often enough. And I really appreciate everything you do to make my life easier."

Mom got teary-eyed and waved her hands in front of her face. "I love you too, baby girl. You are God's gift to a single mother," she replied and drew me back in for another hug.

"Okay, we should get this show on the road before the pizza gets cold," she said finally. "What movie do you want to watch?" she asked as we took our plates to the living room and set them on the tray tables we never used.

"Can we watch *Crazy Rich Asians* again?" I asked. Mom and I had seen it at the movie theatre and we had absolutely adored it. We had watched it again when it came out on the streaming service. We tended to re-watch our favourite movies at regular intervals, and I was hoping there had been enough time since our last viewing for her to agree to it.

"Why not? Set it up while I get a glass of wine," she said and headed into the kitchen.

The movie was as amazing the third time around as it had been the first. It's so romantic. I'm sure this was why Mom wasn't dating anyone and why I had no interest in the boys at school. We've been spoiled by perfect romantic lead males in the movies we watched. I was in no hurry, and Mom shouldn't have to settle!

After the movie, we did the dishes together and Mom asked if I wanted to go for a short stroll to digest all the goodies we ate. I was surprised at this new twist in our routine and started to wonder if this was the outcome of my intending a closer relationship with my mom. I agreed and we headed out for a quick walk around the block. The stars were out and the air was crisp and fragrant with new life as nature woke up.

I went to bed refreshed and eager to visit my remaining alternate selves. Well, the ones from my group anyway. I fell asleep wondering when I'd get to visit selves from other groups and other times.

CHAPTER TWENTY

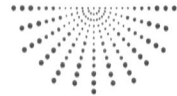

WHEN I ARRIVED AT THE CASTLE, JUNE, JULY, AND AUGUST WERE waiting for me. They were wearing identical lavender silk pyjamas and all three were wearing their hair in a loose braid down their backs. They were indistinguishable and I assumed that meant their lives were rather similar.

One of them held out her hands. This had to be June. I smiled and took them.

She was the violin player. Her life was very much like January's, and I was thrilled to see Gary again.

June went to the same music camp on March break, had the same school schedule. She and her friends were part of a string quartet. Ruby also played the violin, Mark played the cello, and Maggie played the viola. Mark and Maggie made a very cute couple.

They were shockingly good. They practiced every day after school and were often hired to play for various weekend events. All of them would be attending University-level classes in the Fall.

In the blink of an eye, I was back on the sofa taking July's hands. She was the piano player, I was about to ask her about drinking whiskey but I had already been projected into her reality.

The only difference I saw in this life was the instrument and the fact that July was a bit of a loner. I guess that went with the territory; you rarely saw two piano players in an orchestra. Her life was near identical to January's and June's life.

It made me appreciate having a whole hour to eat my lunch. Though I often spent it tutoring or attending remediation, at least I was taking the time to chew and stretch my legs. The whole eating on the bus thing would get old really fast.

On the upside, she had Gary for a stepdad, and I'd seen that hottie Etienne flirting with her at band camp. I could just imagine them doing a heart-wrenching cover of *Shallow* by Lady Gaga and Bradley Cooper. I made a note to suggest it when I saw July next.

Back at the Castle, August was alone. I guessed the other two had places to be. I took her hands and landed in a life similar to February's.

August was on a strict diet and trained daily. She was part of a ballet dance troupe and she spent March break in Toronto, auditioning for a spot at Canada's National Ballet School. The audition went very well and her coach was ecstatic. If she got accepted, she'd attend their Summer Program and decide if she was ready to move to Toronto permanently. The school not only offered dance classes, but a comprehensive elementary, secondary, and post-secondary education.

Mom had to work and did not accompany August to the audition. Their group was staying on campus with their coach and assistant coach. It's the first year Mom had let me take part in the competition. She had said I was too young to leave home for a ballet career before the age of sixteen.

She had only recently broken up with Simon, a guy she had been dating for the past three years. We also discussed a possible move to Toronto. Nana said she'd come with us, seeing as there were more international flights out of Toronto than there were out of Montreal.

If I got in, they'd go on a recon mission when they drove me to camp and we'd see how things go. If Nana moved in with us, or rather if Nana bought the house or condo, Mom could take her time finding a job and settling in. It would make things easier and she'd have someone with her while I was away at school all week. I could come home on weekends and be with them.

I really hoped it worked out for August. It seemed like an amazing opportunity, and she was likely to go with at least one or two of her friends. There were twenty-five dancers in the troupe, but only ten had gone for the audition. August was very close to five of them, Constance, Marie, Lulu, Jason, and Emily.

In addition to their dance lessons during school hours, twice per week, they took Zumba classes after school, and the other three days they did yoga and Pilates. On Saturdays, they trained at the gym.

When the month was up, instead of feeling like a slacker, I felt proud of my selves. They were going after what they wanted and they were killing it. It was very inspiring. As soon as I figured out what I wanted, I'd have great role models to help me achieve my goals.

CHAPTER TWENTY-ONE

SEPTEMBER, OCTOBER, AND NOVEMBER WERE THERE WHEN I OPENED MY eyes. Before I forgot, I asked, to no one in particular, "do you guys know what happens to me in your months?" They all nodded. "How does that work? Did you know before I got here?"

One of them, the science geek, replied, "when someone new joins the group, we get an instant download of their month as soon as they have their Awakening."

"This happens at night, while we're asleep, of course," added the painter.

"How do you know there's been an Awakening?" I asked.

"As soon as you're able to come to the castle at will, or converse with one of us, you are considered Awake."

I mulled this over. Needlepoint was just sitting there, a pleasant smile on her face, stitching away. I admit I was extremely curious about her life. She seemed so tranquil and peaceful.

"Who's first?" I asked, ready to zip through another three months. The experiences felt like they happened much faster now, like they were happening at double speed.

September turned out to be the painter. As I got to know the lives of my other selves, I had been flabbergasted at the number of elite camps in my area. I truly had no idea there were this many arts-study or sports-study programs at my school.

I was therefore not at all surprised to join September at a visual arts camp in Sutton over March break. This one was a day camp, meaning I went home at night. Nana was on taxi duty. She picked me up after breakfast and dropped me off right before dinner.

When school resumed, September's schedule was the same as the others, though she didn't have any after-school activities. When she got home, she would head to the alcove in the dining room that Mom used as a home gym in my timeline. It had the most natural light in the house.

Mom was single in this reality, but she went on dates sometimes on Saturday nights. Nana would come over and we had a girls' night like the ones she had with February. I really should try to initiate these in my reality. Maybe that would inspire Mom to go out more.

There were no famous art school projects in September's future. Every summer, she went to Art camp at the same Visual Arts School where she had her weekly lessons. In the Fall, they had a showing for local artists. Last year, September had sold one of her paintings.

The painting had been a portrait of a child hugging a newly shorn lamb. The Brome-Fair had bought it and were going to use it in next year's promotional poster. It was a great honor and would provide a lot of visibility for her artwork.

September had a few artsy friends, but she was closest to Max, a wood sculptor. They clearly had feelings for each other, but from what I could tell, theirs was a platonic best friend situation. For now, anyway.

They spent all day together at school but split up for their art lessons. Since he lived in Sutton, they didn't see each other after school. They sometimes had video chats, but it was mostly to study or do homework.

September seemed to like being in her own world. When she was painting, it was like she was inside the painting. She did mostly land-scapes, but there were a few portraits of Mom, Nana, and Max.

My favorite was a painting of Clarity Castle. There was an ethereal quality to it that was missing in the others. That was most likely due to the fact that it wasn't a real place. No, that wasn't entirely true. The castle was real, as were those who flocked there to learn, grow, and evolve.

I wasn't an artist, so it was hard to come up with the words. The closest I could come up with was that the painting, like the castle and its surrounding property, was bathed in an extra layer of sunlight. It shimmered in a way that made you feel the blissful vibration coming off of it. Anyone looking at it would instantly want to jump in, like one of Burt's watercolors in Mary Poppins.

* * *

ON THE LAST SATURDAY OF SEPTEMBER, I SPENT THE DAY AT MAX'S. He lived on a sheep farm and his mom had a little shop where they sold wool and knitted items. I guess that explained where I had seen a lamb being shorn. Mom went in for a quick hello and said she'd be back at four to pick me up.

Max had a studio on the second floor of the barn. It was as wide as the barn, with large south-facing windows. I guess I was a frequent guest because one of my paintings rested on an easel by the window. I dropped my bag on the table and went to look at Max's work in progress.

I was surprised. His pieces were usually small, delicate. Like the tiny bird he'd carved for me at Christmas. But this was huge. The log that stood before him was at least two meters long and at least eighty centimetres in diameter. I had no idea what it was going to be, and I knew better than to ask.

It looked like he'd used a saw to cut away the excess wood around the circle he had drawn on the bottom of the log. He must have started this right after camp.

He threw an apron at me and asked if I wanted a cola. Max had the typical artist temperament. He kept odd hours and drank cola at nine in the morning. He wore the exact same outfit every day, blue jeans and a grey t-shirt, to which he added a checkered flannel shirt when it was cold out, like today. He must have an endless supply.

I declined the soda, tied the apron around my waist, and got to work. Not a word was spoken for the next three hours. We worked in companionable silence until Max's mom showed up with a plate of sandwiches, crudités, and her famous chocolate chip cookies.

"Thanks, Mrs. T. I'm starving!" I said as she put the platter on the messy table.

Max hadn't heard his mom come in and only turned when he heard me speak. Wiping his hands on his jeans, he came over and kissed her cheek. "You're the best, Mom."

She ruffled his hair, dislodging a number of wood particles. "Let me know if you need anything else. And maybe crack a window open before you die from the paint fumes," she said as she left.

Max went to the window and flung it open wide. He left it open while we ate. I looked at his work area. He had divided the log into four equal parts and carved V-shaped grooves to separate them. It looked an awful lot like the makings of a totem pole. Still, I made no comment.

He looked at my painting. I wasn't opposed to comments on my work in progress, counter to him. "What do you think?" I asked. He walked over to get a closer look, stared outside, then back at the painting.

"The blue of the Morrissons' house isn't quite right. If you were hoping to match it, that is," he said.

I sighed. "I know. I was trying to match it. Damn," I replied. He had a good eye. "I'll bring some more paints from home next time and try again," I said.

"Don't beat yourself up. You know it's good, or I would have told you," he replied, stuffing a final piece of his brownie in his mouth, then chugging his glass of milk.

Yes, he would have told me. That was the great, but sometimes not so great thing about Max. He always told the truth and never tried to spare anyone's feelings. He didn't go out of his way to hurt anyone, though. It was just his way. I always knew where I stood with Max.

We spent the afternoon working side by side in the studio until Mom came to pick me up. I had never spent so many hours with a friend without talking. But when I left, I felt like I'd said everything I needed to say. For some people, painting, or any art really, lets them express themselves in a truer way than words ever could. Unless you're a writer, I guess. Then words are your art.

CHAPTER TWENTY-TWO

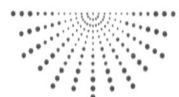

WHEN I OPENED MY EYES, THE GIRL WITH THE LAB COAT WAS THERE. I smiled, I needed to pay attention to this one if I wanted to get into the advanced science classes next year. She introduced herself as October and we were off.

It was not what I was expecting at all. Yes, it was a nerdy science camp. But it wasn't about biology or chemistry. It was about physics. To be specific, this was a robotics and aeronautics camp. And not one lab coat in sight.

A few years ago, the University of Sherbrooke, where the first tournament was held, started offering a week-long camp leading up to the first robotics tournament of the year.

The second tournament was held in Montreal during the Easter break. These were the regional competitions organized by *FIRST Quebec Robotics*, part of an international robotics event. Qualifying teams were then invited to the FIRST LEGO® League World Festival.

Most, but not all, of the students in the Challenge category, for kids fourteen to eighteen, were registered in study-robotics programs in school. October was as well, she was one of only three girls registered in the third-year group of twenty-five students.

At first, when I met Tara and Maelyn, I thought we would become besties and kick the guys' butts. However, we soon found out we were ill-suited both for teamwork and friendship.

October's friends and teammates were Alphonso and Joshua. Both were at camp with her, as were other members of their class. I recognized Joshua from my French class and was glad we had found common ground in this reality. He really was a sweetheart.

The class was divided into two teams, each team had their respective t-shirts, and needed to have two mentors. For our team, we had a teacher as a mentor, and the other was a former participant that now attended college.

Our team made it to the playoff matches but didn't win. Though everything had gone smoothly in the initial trial, one of the wheel bearings wasn't running smoothly and our vehicle went just a little off track. It was enough to add a few seconds to the final lap. It was easily corrected, and we would get another chance at the Montreal event next month.

Back at school, October spent two afternoons per week learning science, engineering, and technology skills. Other than competing in tournaments, the program was meant to lead students to STEM education programs after high school.

October's life was otherwise pretty much like mine. She spent the bulk of her evenings at home, with Mom, doing homework and studying for tests.

Needless to say, she was nailing the math, science, and technology classes. She put less effort into her French and English classes and her results were the bare minimum required to stay in the program, which was a seventy-five percent average.

Her main hobby was assembling the famous Scandinavian bricks. In the room we used for storage downstairs in my own timeline, she had a huge collection. Two folding tables were set up. One was covered with an impressive town, complete with a robotic train and a remote-controlled helicopter, while the other was used for assembling projects and various sorting trays. Under the second table were four rolling carts, each with three drawers where pieces were sorted not by colour but by category: people parts, regular bricks, moving parts, and others I wouldn't be able to describe.

She, Alphonso, and Karl spent every Saturday afternoon holed up in this room without windows. When Mom would come down to check on us, she would ask us to open the fan as it was getting a bit rank in there.

They never worked on competition stuff in here. They just created, for the fun of it. Alphonso and Karl had their own set-ups at home, but neither was as expansive as mine.

It's fascinating to me that my other selves could have such a wide range of strengths and interests, yet still be me. I mean, they are obviously their own people. But as surprising as each new reality seemed at first, I could totally see myself in it even when I wouldn't choose it.

This was to be expected. The choices they made were based on minute differences in how they reacted or responded to opportunities or events, mostly in childhood. And a lot of it centred around what Mom did or didn't do, or whether my dad or some other figure was around.

I never thought Mom's love life had anything to do with me, but clearly her dating Gary had led to a bunch of musical realities. And so far, Dad being around had not turned out all that great, sad as that may be.

CHAPTER TWENTY-THREE

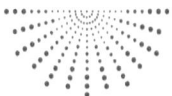

NOVEMBER, WEARING A BLACK KIMONO, WAS STANDING NEAR THE fireplace. I didn't remember a martial arts enthusiast from my first or second visit. Then I saw the bangs. Emo Girl!

She was scowling at me, visibly uncomfortable with my staring. She stalked over and clasped my right arm like we were warriors, her hand gripping my upper arm. I didn't have time to voice a snarky comment before I landed in her world.

I was expecting her to be holed up in her room, writing poetry and listening to sad music. I remembered being a little confused upon seeing her that first time. How was an emo girl at Clarity Castle? Wouldn't all the negative emotions keep her from accessing her 'Knowing' as the teacher called it?

As far as I knew, there was no such thing as an emo camp. Had I not seen Emo Girl and Writer Girl in the same room, I would have put my money on them being one and the same.

I was wrong. On Sunday evening, Nana dropped her off at an industrial-looking building in Drummondville. She went in, signed some forms, kissed November goodbye and said she'd be back to pick her up on Saturday. The counsellor assured her that I was in good hands and that the week spent in individual and group therapy would do me a world of good.

Where the heck was Mom? Why was Nana signing forms? I was suddenly very scared. So was November and it wiped the scowl from her face.

After Nana left, I was provided with a stack of items: bedding, a towel, and two ninja suits. If they'd been orange jumpsuits, I wouldn't have been surprised. The place screamed juvenile detention center even though the sign outside read 'You 2.0 - A Center For Troubled Teens.'

They searched my backpack and removed unauthorized items, namely my cell phone, tablet, and some snacks Nana had packed. These were placed in a bag I would retrieve at the end of the week. A sturdy matron in a black jumpsuit then requested I remove all jewelry and accessories and handed me two facial wipes to remove my makeup. One would not have been enough.

A girl my age was waiting for me. The counsellor introduced her as Kim, saying she would show me to the room she and I would share. On the way, Kim explained that new recruits we always paired with an established one. *Recruits?* This sounded more and more like boot camp. I couldn't imagine this emo girl misbehaving to the point of being sent to reform school.

"Make your bed, put on your uniform, and stow your things in the dresser," she said, pleasantly enough. When I just stood there, she seemed to understand I was hoping for some privacy in order to change. The room did not have a private bathroom.

She went out in the hall and said, "I'll wait for you here. You have five minutes," before closing the door. I was relieved to see there were no locks or bars on the door. There was, however, no window in the room either.

I quickly made my bed, changed, and put my things away. I was debating what to do about shoes. I remembered then that Kim had been barefoot and followed her lead. When I opened the door, she nodded and said, "come with me."

We went down a hall with identical doors on either side, then through double doors to another hall that branched out in three directions. We turned right. It looked a lot like a hospital. I was worried. So was November.

We became especially worried when we stopped in front of a door marked 'Dr. Eva Rivers.' Kim knocked on the door, waited a moment, then opened the door.

"Hello Dr. Rivers," she said with a smile. She was standing with her hands clasped behind her back, feet hip-distance apart. *At ease, soldier,* I thought to myself.

"Hello, Kim. Who do you have here?" asked the doctor, rising from her desk and coming to meet us on the other side of it.

"This is Clare Knox, my roommate for the week," replied Kim.

"Thank you, Kim. I'll take it from here," replied Dr. Rivers.

Dismissed, Kim gave a half bow to each of them and left the room.

"Hello, Clare. I'm Dr. Eva Rivers," she said to me, hand outstretched and smiling.

I was unable to smile, anxious as I was, but I did manage to shake her hand and offer a weak, "Hello Doctor."

"Don't look so worried. Here, have a seat and we'll begin," she urged, motioning to one of the chairs in front of her desk.

I sat primly in the seat while she looked over what was presumably my file. Eventually, she said, "I see you've been living with your grandmother since your parents died in January." She looked to me for confirmation. *What?* All of a sudden, I can feel November's pain and sadness. It's true. I nodded. *What happened?*

"Your grandmother has provided us with your latest report card, and the assessment made by the school psychologist. It appears that though your schoolwork has not suffered, you've retreated from your social circle and spend most of your time alone. Your guardian reports she often hears you crying in your room, but you refuse to talk about it with her."

"You also declined weekly sessions with a therapist. When your grandmother grew worried, the school counsellor suggested an after-school activity that might help you channel some of your emotions. This, you did not decline and have never missed a karate class. Your instructor says you have a natural ability and have improved at an impressive pace," she explained.

At this, November bristled. *They've even talked to my karate instructor. Is nothing sacred?* she wondered. I agreed, this was getting creepy. They knew way too much about me.

"What if I told you I could cure your melancholy in a snap?" she asked, closing the file and looking intently at me.

Her gaze was like the high beams of a car to a deer, blinding yet impossible to look away from. My first thought was drugs or electrochock therapy. Did they still do that? Was it legal?

I must have looked horrified because Dr. Rivers immediately continued by saying, "no, nothing sinister like what you seem to be imagining," she chuckled.

"Your parents were operatives for a secret intelligence unit of the armed forces called the Canadian Special Operations Forces Command. They died in an undercover operation that went south," she said and waited for me to process this.

"What?" I said, but what I meant was W*hat. The. Actual. Fuck?*

Expecting this incredulity, she produced two glossy eight-by-ten pictures of Mom and Dad, wearing standard army fatigues. I picked up Mom's first. Her hair was tied back in a severe ponytail and her unsmiling face looked like that of a stranger. Tears welled up in my eyes as I picked up Dad's picture. He looked a lot like he did when he was in jail. Tan, lean, and a little mean.

Something snapped inside me, and I dropped the pictures back on her desk.

"You mean they didn't die in a car crash on the way back from a show in Montreal?" I demanded, denial giving way to anger.

"No. They were ambushed while retrieving sensitive information in the alley behind the theatre. While they were meeting with their informant, an incendiary device was placed on their car," she said.

A second ticked by. Two. Three.

"They died from a car bomb?" I cried, eyes wide.

She nodded. "Technically, they weren't in the car. They were thrown some fifteen feet by the blast when they touched the handle.

They died from the ensuing injuries," she specified. "Would you like to see the report? So you know I'm telling the truth?" she asked, holding out another folder.

I wanted to say no. That would make it real. But they were dead anyway, might as well know the truth. I held out my hand and she gave me the folder. I braced myself for gruesome pictures, but there was only a picture of the crime scene after the bodies had been taken away. As I read about third-degree burns, broken ribs, and a shattered pelvis, I grew sick.

Like she was reading my mind, or perhaps the colour of my face, Dr. Rivers extended a trash can. I took it and immediately let go of my dinner and my emotions. I started sobbing uncontrollably, then laughing hysterically. When I was done, she took the can, passed me a tissue, and told me I could freshen up in her private bathroom while she disposed of the can.

I went through the door she showed me and splashed some water on my face, washed my hands and gargled with water. When I came out, the can was gone, and Dr. Rivers handed me a bottle of water.

"How do you feel?" she asked, curious.

"Angry," I replied and found I was seething. How could Mom and Dad have kept this from me? How dare they die and leave me alone with nothing but questions.

Dr. Rivers smiled in satisfaction and said, "See, I told you I could cure your melancholy!"

CHAPTER TWENTY-FOUR

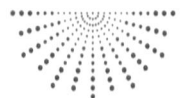

THERE WAS A KNOCK AT THE DOOR AND AFTER A PAUSE, KIM CAME BACK in. Dr. Rivers asked Kim to explain what they did here.

"New recruits are assessed upon arrival. If they are deemed to be suitable candidates for the program, they will begin training. If they are not suitable candidates, they will attend workshops and therapy sessions relevant to their situation and return home at the end of the week," replied Kim, standing in that quasi-military stance.

"What kind of assessment and what kind of training are we talking about?" I asked, more out of curiosity than any real interest. The whole thing was bonkers. I'd attend the mandatory workshops and therapy and go home to have an interesting conversation with Nana.

"Assessment has already begun. The contents of your file are the first part of the screening. Your reaction to the existence of the secret task force and your parents' involvement is also being analyzed," replied Dr. Rivers.

"And then?" I asked, aware that my question had not yet been answered.

"There will be a series of physical tests, language proficiency, performance under stress, that kind of thing," said Kim.

"Can I refuse to be tested?" I asked. I don't know how much

November and I had in common, but I would likely fail most of the physical tests.

"I'm afraid not. It's mandatory for all camp attendees. Some of the results will go into the report provided for the parents or guardians. All of the results are sent to HQ, especially for legacy recruits," said Dr. Rivers.

"Legacy?" I asked.

"Children of operatives are automatically tested," explained Kim.

"Tell me about the training," I said, directing my question to Kim in the hopes I'd get an answer this time.

"You must have seen CIA, MI6, and FBI movies or TV shows, right?" she said. I rolled my eyes. "It's pretty much like that, only for teenagers. I mean, this facility only trains teenagers. Adult candidates are assessed and trained in other facilities," said Kim.

"Wait, so this is basically a school for spy kids?" I asked with a chuckle.

"Teenagers are extremely resilient, they adapt more quickly to change than do most adults. They also have less resistance to learning new things or new ways of doing things," said Dr. Rivers.

This was unreal. But there was clearly no way out of here for the next seven days. As the saying went, the only way out was through.

"How long does the training last?" I asked, wondering what I'd be in for if they deemed me suitable.

"That depends on when you begin and how much time you devote to it. At your age, if you came here only on weekends and school holidays, basic training would likely take about five years. However, if you attend school here full time, you would finish your training at the same time as high school," explained Kim.

"Then what?" I asked.

"Most students go on to the next phase of training, which also includes a university degree. We follow the Canadian curriculum, there would be no CEGEP. However, some students decide to start taking minor field assignments while they continue their education in the normal way," said Kim.

"You mean like the army reserve?" I asked. I remember seeing a flyer about that at school as a career path.

"Yes, exactly!" said Kim.

"So, this is basically like going into the army," I said.

"With an added twist," said Kim.

"Do you think you have enough information for now? It's almost time for lights out," said Dr. Rivers.

I looked at the clock on the wall. It was eight forty-five. My brain couldn't take much more of this anyway, so I said I was fine for now.

"Alright, Kim will explain the schedule and walk you through it tomorrow. Good night, Kim. Good night, Clare. And welcome to *You two point oh!*" she said in a voice that was way too chipper to be reassuring.

I'd probably leave here with a lobotomy.

Back in our room, Kim laid out the daily schedule. Five am wake-up, warm-up and training session, showers, breakfast, workshops, lunch, outdoor activities, therapy sessions, journal writing (or other individual activity), dinner, free time, lights out at nine pm.

I blew out a breath. I was exhausted just hearing about it.

"Grab your towel and toiletries, I'll show you where the bathroom is," said Kim.

On the way, she explained that the hall lights dimmed but stayed on at night in case I needed to go to the bathroom in the middle of the night. She also said there were hall cameras and that the double doors at either end of the hall were locked for our safety. No one was allowed to enter a room that wasn't theirs, ever. If we wanted to spend time with someone, it would be in the common rooms during free time.

I was relieved to see individual bathroom and shower stalls. When Mom had taken me to the gym once, everyone showered in the same room. I wasn't down with that. And I'd seen enough movies to worry about privacy.

We brushed our teeth, washed up, and put on our pyjamas. There were other girls in the bathroom and Kim introduced me, though I was too nervous to remember any of the names. In the hall on the way back, everyone was smiling and saying goodnight like this was a sorority. Maybe it was.

"Are there boys here?" I asked when we were getting in bed.

"I was wondering when you would ask!" said Kim with a laugh. I waited, saying nothing. "Yes, but not in this hall. Boys are in another hall. Most activities are co-ed, as are the instructors," she said moving around in her bed until she was comfortable.

"Tell the truth, am I going to die here?" I asked, feigning humour but really interested in the answer.

She burst out laughing, and replied, "of course not, silly. It's just like camp, a very active camp."

"So, it's not going to be like training for Dauntless?" I asked, my voice barely above a whisper. The lights had turned out.

"Only a little," she whispered back.

Shit.

* * *

THE WEEK WAS GRUELLING IN WAYS I CANNOT DESCRIBE. I LEFT 'CAMP' with an offer to join their training program, either part-time or full-time. They gave Nana a bunch of fake flyers about the school and told her I had shown so much promise, I would be receiving a full scholarship.

Before I left, Dr. Rivers said I could attend up to three weekend training sessions before I made up my mind. That would give me enough time to discuss it with Nana, decide if this was a good fit for me, and make arrangements if I decided to transfer mid-year.

Nana was very impressed, both with the scholarship and with the report she had received. I had made a complete three-sixty and was now a happy, well-adjusted teenager ready to reach my full potential.

On the drive home, Nana asked what I thought about it all. I told her honestly that I was considering transferring there full time, but that I wanted to sleep on it first.

"That's a very mature decision, young lady. I'm so proud of you," she said. "And I'm sure your parents are very proud of you, wherever they are," she added.

I just bet they were.

CHAPTER TWENTY-FIVE

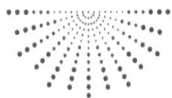

I OPENED MY EYES, MY HEART STILL PUMPING FROM THE SURPRISE NIGHT exercise, and sagged into the sofa in relief. I most definitely did not want to switch places with November. I patted myself down, checking for sore muscles and new bruises, but they were gone. Sadly, so had my lean and toned body. I was back to my usual mushy self.

Only then did I notice someone was in the room with me. It was needlepoint girl. December. When she noticed me looking at her, she smiled and put down her needlework.

"You don't say much," I said to her.

"God gave us two eyes and two ears, but only one mouth," she replied, as cryptic as the Dalai Lama. She seemed so nice that I didn't want to inadvertently offend her with a response.

I extended my hands to her in invitation. She got up from her seat and came to sit next to me on the sofa. She took one of my hands and cradled it in both of hers.

"Don't worry, it all turns out okay in the end," she said soothingly.

* * *

I WAS ON A PLANE, SITTING NEXT TO NANA. IT APPEARED WE WERE ON our way to Spain, specifically to Granada. She and December were both doing needlepoint and wearing identical serene expressions. I was starting to panic again. *Where's Mom? Why wasn't she on the trip with us?* December's memories flushed my brain.

Mom had been dating a guy named Simon for the last three years. He didn't live with us, but he often took me and Mom on various outings, and he came with us on our yearly family vacation with Nana. I liked him, he was nice. However, he died in a stupid skiing accident in January and Mom's been a mess. Though Nana helped out as much as she could, I had to pick up the slack at home.

Since I was intent on making the honour roll in every possible subject, the level of stress I had been experiencing got dangerously high and my homeroom teacher suggested I speak with a counsellor. She suggested activities I might do to help channel my energy and emotions. Since I already had so much to do, and she was insisting I pick one, I had chosen needlepoint to placate her.

It was offered as a lunchtime activity twice per week. It gave me a great excuse not to hang with my friends. They meant well, but I was tired of talking about my problems and much too tired to hear about theirs. My brain was so stuffed with all the goals I wanted to achieve and all the chores I needed to get done at home.

The activity was led by the school psychologist. When I saw her from the door, I balked and considered leaving. But she had spotted me and checked her list for my name. I reluctantly gave it to her and entered the room.

There were about twenty kids in here, boys and girls, as well as a handful of staff members. The only person I recognized was Valerie, a girl from my French class. She smiled at me and nodded to the seat next to her.

Mrs. Reynolds was beckoning me. She gave me a bag and invited me to take a seat.

"I'd like to welcome our new members to needlepoint class. You may think that needlepoint has gone out of style decades ago. But you may be surprised that needlepoint, crocheting, and knitting have made comebacks as mindfulness practices," she said.

While she spoke, Valerie opened the bag I was still holding and laid out the contents on my lap. She urged me to hold the ring. She then took her kit and started stitching. I looked around and everyone but the newbies was stitching. One of the staff members and two other students were holding the ring the way I was. Weird.

"Mindfulness is the process of slowing down and taking time to focus our full attention on where we are, and what we are thinking, feeling, and doing in the present moment. It's the practice of being aware of, and engaged with, our emotions and actions as they occur, accepting them without judgement."

"When we are aware of our feelings at a given time, we create the opportunity to interact with others thoughtfully, as opposed to simply reacting or acting out reflexively. Mindfulness is an enormous piece of self-care and wellness, particularly given how negatively stress can affect our health," she went on.

I realized that stitching was a mostly silent activity.

"How does stitching relate to mindfulness? When we engage in a task with our hands it allows our minds to wander, or just be. The work itself has a meditative, rhythmic quality to it, and it allows our thoughts and feelings to percolate. We can stitch while a thorny issue simmers. Often, at the end of the time spent stitching, we have arrived at some resolution or are at least better able to tolerate the ambiguity of the situation. The kinetic aspect of stitching gives our brains a little space to pause, reflect, and observe our emotions without judgement," she concluded.

She then went around to answer questions. Valerie placed the provided canvas onto the frame. It wasn't a colloquial country land-scape. Painted on the canvas were the words 'Be. Here. Now.' How apt. She showed me how to thread the needle and knot the thread. The threads in my bag had various colours but were all precut to the appropriate length. She explained this first needlepoint wasn't about making it pretty. It was about learning to stitch and staying present. I started with the basic continental stitch and realized how easy this was.

After about fifteen minutes, Mrs. Reynolds came over and praised my work. She asked how I was feeling, and I had to admit it was the first time I'd felt relaxed in a while. Valerie stayed quiet, other than to provide pointers now and then.

Some students had moved away to chat as they stitched. Others were listening to music through earbuds. But the atmosphere was as Zen as if we'd been doing a yoga or meditation class.

I was surprised when the bell rang and it was time to go back to class. Mrs. Reynolds said we were allowed to stitch during class if that helped us stay calm and focused. She also mentioned that there were knitting and crocheting groups we could try if stitching wasn't our thing.

At first, I was too embarrassed to stitch in class. But when the next French class rolled around, I saw Valerie stitching during the teacher's explanation and followed suit. Within a week, I realized that stitching was not only great at staying calm, but I found it led to easy solutions to my school tasks.

Nonetheless, Nana was worried about me. She requested permission to take me out of school an extra week after March break. It had to go through Mom of course, but both the principal and the counsellor agreed. Since the semester ended in February, I wouldn't miss anything major and could make it up when I got back.

Mom was seeing a therapist and, when she went back to work, she hired a part-time housekeeper. Nana assured me Mom was going to be okay and it was time for me to take a well-deserved break.

And that is why we were flying to Granada. Intent on providing me with a once-in-a-lifetime experience, Nana had enrolled us in a two-week walk to Santiago de Compostella. It was one of the Camino routes, a lesser-known one called the Andalusian Camino.

I had at first been skeptical about Nana and me being able to walk the one hundred and sixty-three kilometres to Santiago, but when she showed me the pictures and mentioned the average temperature would be about fifteen degrees Celsius, I was in.

We were technically part of a group tour, but the Camino is known as something you do by yourself, for yourself. Walking with others wasn't recommended as each might not have the same pace. I was pretty sure Nana was fitter than me and we'd be fine.

The route was divided into eleven stages. We had a set number of kilometres to do every day, which we completed at our own pace, and met up with the others at the day's chosen accommodations. Once there, we could do our own thing, or join the group to visit the town, or for the nightly meal.

Nana had gotten us each a European SIM card so we could keep in touch with Mom and each other should we lose track of each other on the trail. After the first day, I understood why this was a good thing, and how it wasn't a big deal to let a fifteen-year-old Canadian girl wander on her own in the south of Spain.

For one thing, there were few people on the Camino in March. For another, pilgrims—as those who walk the Way of Santiago were called —were treated with the utmost respect. Townspeople would offer food, water, or a place to rest along the way. And finally, because I was the only person in our group that was under sixty, I was now the mascot everyone wanted to keep an eye on. But at a safe, respectful distance.

I can't say I had any big revelations on the way, no great spiritual awakening. However, I had never been so at peace, so *in the moment*, other than when I was stitching. There was nothing to do but walk and drink in the scenery. The Andalusian countryside was breathtaking. I had often seen pictures of Tuscany on the internet, but this was better.

Every day the number of kilometres increased a little. By day nine, we were averaging twenty kilometres a day and I barely noticed a difference. At the end of the day, I was happy to remove my shoes and put on my flip-flops. But I hadn't gotten any blisters and I wasn't sore or even tired when I woke up.

I took about a gazillion pictures and would upload the best ones to my Instagram account at night when we had access to Wi-Fi. I'd shoot a few extra ones to Mom via email but that was the scope of my screen-related activities.

When we finally reached Santiago, I couldn't believe we had basically walked across Spain. We stayed an extra day there and visited Finistere where the zero-kilometre marker stood, called the End of the World.

The weather was cooler here, but I didn't ever want to leave. I wanted to move to this little coastal village and swim in the sea every day. Alas, real life was calling, and I felt ready to conquer it.

I came home tan, rested, and fully infected with the travel bug. Nana promised we'd plan a special trip over the summer now that she knew I was such a great travel companion. I was so Zen, I easily caught up with all my schoolwork when I went back to school. And it was only after my first exam, for which I had not nearly studied as much I was used to, that I saw that my whole life had changed. Whether it was the needlepoint or the Camino, there was no way I was going back to the old me.

CHAPTER TWENTY-SIX

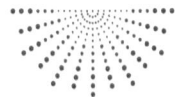

My hands felt empty when I returned to the yellow room. December smiled and gave me her needlepoint frame. Just holding it made me feel ecstatic. I would definitely look into this stitching thing. And I made a note to ask Nana to take me to Spain this summer. I had to do that trip for myself. I was just sitting there, all Zenlike when the Teacher appeared.

"Now that you've accessed everyone's memories, we can assemble for the ritual," she said.

For a minute there, I panicked. Ritual? Images from gothic movies from the nineties flooded my brain. I remembered I was at Clarity Castle then, and that it was probably only a group meditation around a circle of crystals.

I wasn't that far off. The teacher took my hand and we immediately appeared in a windowless room in the basement. It was a circular room with twelve portraits of each of us hanging on the walls. September had painted them, and I frowned to see Writer scribbling in her notebook under the word March. As I made my way to stand in front of it the way the others had, I was about to remark on the error, but September only winked at me and told me to just go with it. I shrugged and let it go. This wasn't about me, it was about April.

There was indeed a circle of crystals in the middle. The teacher, and what I assumed was her Guide, went to stand inside careful not to disturb the perimeter. Once everyone was in place, the Guide invited April to join them in the circle. She was then asked to voice her intention.

"I would like to go back to the sixteenth of January. That's when the newspapers said my dad and his colleagues were approached with the opportunity. I hope to convince him, with my precognition of events, not to do it and, if possible, have him convince the others not to do it either, or at least to steer clear of them should they proceed anyway," she said.

"You are aware that your father and all other implicated have free will and that your intervention may not yield the desired results, that the current outcome may be the most advantageous one, and that you will have to deal with the new outcome, whatever it may be, is that correct?" asked the Guide.

April said yes. The Guide then faced each of us in turn and asked if we agreed with April's intention. We all said yes. We were asked to come as close to the circle as possible without touching it and hold hands. April took her place among us. For a minute, I thought how creepy it was that I was standing in a circle with eleven—thirteen if you counted the Teacher and the Guide—of my lookalikes.

We joined hands and January shared a vision of the sixteenth of January. It was a Saturday. Mom had taken Penny to her swimming lessons. Dad and I were alone at home. It was the perfect time to have the initial discussion.

The floor seemed to vibrate a little. I felt heat coming from April's hand on my right and then she was gone, my hand grasping air.

"Did it work?" I blurted out. I immediately apologized and put a hand on my mouth.

That broke the spell, and everyone stopped holding hands. The Teacher laughed and told me not to worry about it. Though it was a ritual, it wasn't sacred or anything. It was more of a symbolic ritual whose purpose was to teach us the value of doing our homework,

voicing clear intentions, and taking responsibility for the conse-
quences.

"April was successful in returning to the requested date. To know
whether she accomplished her goal, you'll need to search your memories of her reality. They will already have changed," she said.

"As quick as that?" I asked. Then, I quickly added a "never mind"
before she could remind me that past and present were illusions.

As everyone left, or I should say disappeared back into their lives, I
asked the Teacher for a moment.

"You said this is a symbolic ritual. When can we make a jump back
or forward in time, or in another timeline on our own?" I asked.

"Did you find a more suitable reality on your travels?" she asked
with a smile.

"No, I'm just curious. As you predicted, I liked certain aspects of
everyone's lives and will be implementing a few changes in my own as
a result," I answered.

"Once you've implemented those changes and maintained a high
vibration for a few months, you'll be transferred to a group of six,
then three, then two. After that, you'll be on your own. How long you
stay with each group will depend on the speed of your growth and the
strength of your desires," she said.

I nodded slowly at this. It was still a vague answer, but I guessed it
meant I wasn't going anywhere for the time being.

I pointed to my portrait. "What does September know about me
that I don't? Does this mean I become a writer?" I asked.

"There are two ways you can find out. The first is to ask
September for a glimpse of your reality. The second is to just wait and
see," she said with a wink. Her smile made me think she was
goading me.

"But doesn't me seeing the portrait already put me on that path?" I
asked. I was starting to get this whole time-space continuum thing. By
knowing I would be a writer in the future, whether or not I saw a
vision of it, the very idea would activate that aspect of my life. Sure, I
got high marks in all my written assignments, both in French and

English. But I'd never seen myself as a writer, per se. Then again, I'd never seen myself as anything, really.

"Remember that everyone has free will. If you don't like the idea, you can choose another. But when asked what your skill was upon arrival, you answered 'worrying.' You can't fault us for wanting to give you a nudge," she said and gave me an actual nudge with her shoulder before leaving me alone in the ritual room.

I didn't like the idea of staying alone in the basement of any building, let alone a castle.

But I wasn't ready to wake up just yet, so I made an intention to go to the lake. It would be nice to sit alone on the bench and look at the water for as long as I wanted, and not worry about getting a sunburn.

CHAPTER TWENTY-SEVEN

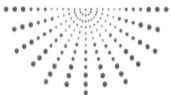

I WOKE UP AT HOME. PERHAPS I HAD OVERSTAYED MY WELCOME AT THE Castle. What day was it? My phone confirmed that it's Sunday and a little past nine in the morning. I sniffed the air. Bacon. And waffles!

I abandoned my phone without checking the feeds and rushed out of my room.

"Good morning, honey," said Mom, taking the bacon out of the oven. She barely had time to say, "you're just in time!" when the smoke alarm started to wail. I grabbed the piece of cardboard we kept on hand for just this purpose and waved it at the offending device. Once quieted, I went over to give Mom our good morning hug.

"Smells good," I said and headed for the bathroom.

When I came out, she'd set the table and we had our feast.

"Did you see Nana's first pictures from Casablanca?" she asked, sipping her coffee.

"No, I fell like a log last night, and the smell of waffles distracted me this morning. I'll check after breakfast," I replied.

Mom refused to make pancakes, waffles, or any kind of baking unless I helped with the dishes. She'd been busy while I slept. She had made muffins and cookies for the week and there was a mountain of bowls and pans waiting for us.

My child labour completed, I went to my room to check on the feeds and plan that bike ride for after lunch. Mel had beaten me to it. We were all set for a one o'clock meet-up at the lake.

I hit the books for the rest of the morning, had lunch, and set out for fun with my friends. Meanwhile, Mom went hiking with a friend. She said she wanted to make the most of it before they closed the trails for mud season. With the warm temperatures, the ice and snow were melting more rapidly this year.

When I got home around four, she wasn't back. She must have gotten a ride from her friend because the car was in the drive. I checked the weekly menu and saw she had salmon planned for tonight. That was easy enough. I pre-heated the oven, sprinkled some maple-chipotle seasoning on the salmon, and started on the salad while the fish was baking.

When I heard a car door, I peeked out the kitchen window to see if it was Mom or another delivery. Mom was really into online shopping. I saw Mom, but she was not alone. It was Mom and a dude!

It must have been a date because the guy leapt out of the car and made a mad dash around to open Mom's door. He was moving so fast, I couldn't get a good look at his face. She must have been anticipating this because she took her time gathering her things. When he opened the door for her, Mom blushed and giggled like a schoolgirl. I mean, I couldn't hear her, but I knew what a giggle looked like.

When she was out, he opened the back door and grabbed her water pack. There was an awkward moment when she tried to take it from him, and he simultaneously tried to place it on her shoulders. I laughed out loud then hid in case they'd heard me.

When I rose up to spy on them some more, they were out of my line of sight. Within minutes, Mom was walking into the house and Romeo's car was pulling out of the driveway.

The oven was beeping, and I grabbed the mittens. Mom quickly removed her shoes and ran to fan the smoke detector as I opened the oven door.

"Honey, you made dinner?" she asked, kissing my temple. "I'm starving. Sorry I'm late, it was so nice we took the long way down the mountain," she said, washing her hands and carrying the plates to the table.

I waited until we'd sat down to eat before grilling her.

"So... What's his name?" I asked innocently.

"Whose name?" she asked, just as innocently.

"The dude, Mom!" I said, laughing at the face she was making. I could tell she was torn. She wanted to tell me about the date because it had just happened and she needed to tell someone about it. On the other hand, the Perfect Parent Handbook clearly stated you should discuss your love life with your kids only when it was serious enough to introduce them to a potential life partner.

"Mom, I'm almost sixteen. Most of my friends are dating or have boyfriends. I can handle you telling me about a hiking date!" I said, trying to keep a straight face.

She took a huge bite of her salad and chewed for a really long time. Then she took a long sip of wine. I was dying to know, and my leg started to shake impatiently under the table. What if his name was Simon? Would he die in an accident? The ski season was over, but there was always mountain biking, rock climbing, or base jumping! Mom liked outdoorsy types. Well, this one did. The alternate versions of her clearly had a wide range of types.

Finally, she put her glass down and said, "his name is Gary."

It took everything I had not to jump up and down on the spot or whoop with joy. I was, however, unable to hide a smile. I had to focus. It might not be him.

"What does he do?" I asked in singsong, pumping my eyebrows.

She laughed and resumed eating. "He's a staff photographer for a company that publishes a dozen or so trade magazines," she said.

Holy Guacamole! It was *him*. It was my Gary. Our Gary. I was so excited I had to excuse myself and go to the bathroom where I promptly danced a celebratory jig and pumped my arms in the air as if I'd just scored a touchdown. *Yes, yes, yes!*

I flushed, washed my hands and came back to the dinner table where, as nonchalantly as I could, I asked, "how did you meet?"

"It's the funniest thing. You know that dating app you've been at me to join? Well, Michelle has also been bugging me to join. So I did, just to shut her up. The app lets you know if you have friends in common and I like that feature. It's kind of like getting references for a job interview," she said.

It was just like Mom to look at dating like a human resource project.

"Anyway, Gary is friends with Michelle! So, I ask her what's wrong with Gary? Why hadn't she tried setting me up with him before? She'd introduced me to every single male in her vicinity until now. Why stop there?"

We'd finished dinner and Mom suggested we made s'mores for dessert out by the fire pit. While we were putting the dishes into the dishwasher, I said, "and then?"

"She said she hadn't known Gary was single. He'd been dating another woman as far as she knew," Mom replied.

"No!" I said.

"So, Michelle asked her husband about it. Gary is his friend. It turned out they had broken up just after Christmas and Michelle's husband hadn't thought to mention it."

We went out with the ingredients and Mom got the fire started. We sat in the chairs and waited for it to light fully.

"Wow! And how long have you been dating? It can't have been long unless you've been sneaky about it," I asked.

"This was our second date. Or I should say our first *real* date. The first one we only met for coffee to see if we liked each other in real life. He was on assignment in the Townships this week, and I had a break between interviews, so we made it happen," she explained.

I started putting marshmallows on my double roasting stick while Mom started separating the crackers and the chocolate bar and divided them onto our plates.

"I guess it went well if you decided to see each other again. How did it go today?" I asked, trying not to sound like I had a vested interest in the outcome of their date. Mom didn't seem to notice. I wasn't asking any weird or overly personal questions.

"It went well. He's a very good photographer and he loves being outdoors. I was a little self-conscious about all the pictures I posted on Facebook, but he thought they were good," she replied.

"Are you going to see him again?" I asked, squishing the marsh-mallow between the crackers, licking the melted chocolate before it hit the ground.

"Yes, we've planned a longer hike for next Saturday and then maybe go out to dinner. Will you be okay on your own? Nana won't be home yet. Maybe you can invite your friends over?" she said, unsure.

"OMG, Mom! I'm old enough to stay home alone on a Saturday night," I said, pretending to be affronted. No need to mention I *would* invite my friends over because I actually was afraid to stay home alone. I had had no practice, she never went anywhere! "But I'll see what Mel, Julie, and Sam have going on," I added breezily.

"Wonderful!" she said, looking relieved. Poor Mom, worried about leaving her baby home alone.

We stayed by the fire long after we'd reached our limit of s'mores, just staring at the flames. I was pretty sure we were both thinking about Gary. Her, wondering if it would work out. Me, hoping it would.

Wait a minute, I thought. There was a way I could find out if it went beyond the third date. By the same token, I could have a peek at what my life would look like in a few months' time. I wasn't sure how to go about it, though. If I called on September, I think I'd be a passenger in her reality, the way I had been in January's and April's.

If I wanted access to September's memories of my reality, which happened in the future for me but the past for her, I think I needed to see her at the Castle. But how did I make sure she was there tonight?

I got up abruptly and Mom jumped. "Sorry, I just remembered I forgot to do a final read-through for an assignment I have to hand in tomorrow," I said.

Mom checked her watch and asked me to get her book. She would read until the fire died down. I went to get her book and said good-night, in case I needed more time to check in with September.

I put on pyjamas, brushed my teeth, and set my alarm. It was only eight-thirty but I wanted to get these out of the way in case my errand took longer to accomplish. At Clarity Castle, there was no time and it didn't matter how long things took, so I wasn't sure how this would go.

I sat in my bed cross-legged and closed my eyes. I took a deep breath, cleared my mind, and called out to September in my mind.

"Hey, what's up," she replied instantly, presumably from her mind as well.

"I'd like to get a peek at what's going to happen in September. That's allowed, right?" I asked. It was easier if I just imagined she was standing in front of me in the yellow room.

"Yes, of course, that's why we're in the same group," she replied.

"How does that work? Do you show me now? Do we make an appointment? Do we meet at the Castle?" I asked.

"We need to be at the Castle. If it's only a peek, and not a whole month, then we could meet there anytime. Otherwise, it has to be at night," she explained.

"If it was, how would I make sure you, or anybody else, would be there?" I asked.

"You'd ask, like this, beforehand," she said.

"Ok, when would you be free?" I asked.

"I can meet now if you want. Mom's reading by the fire and I'm already in bed," she said.

"Same," I exclaimed, amazed how our lives were mirrored even five months apart. April and September both were good times to enjoy an outdoor fire. "Did you have s'mores too?" I asked. She laughed and said no because her mom had cut out sugar so all they had was peppermint tea. I sympathized and hoped that wasn't part of the coming attractions for me. We agreed to meet at the Castle.

Instantly, we were both in the yellow room.

CHAPTER TWENTY-EIGHT

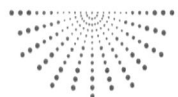

It's kind of awkward, but we hugged when we saw each other. I was dying to talk to someone about all this and for a good fifteen minutes, that's what we did. I asked how her life had changed since discovering the Castle and her awakening.

"My art has improved a lot, and so have my relationships. Do you remember Max?" she asked.

"The quiet woodworking hottie?" I asked with a wink. She blushed.

"Yes, him. Well, as comfortable as we were doing our art in companionable silence, I wanted him to open up to me, you know, talk. Now, he's always sharing his innermost thoughts and feelings. I sometimes wish he'd shut up so I can work," she said.

"Be careful what you wish for. Got it," I replied and we both burst out laughing.

"But seriously, it brought us closer and things have progressed to where we're almost dating," she said.

"Almost?" I asked.

"Though we've talked about everything else, we haven't had 'the talk.' We hold hands at school, and he's kissed me on the lips a few times, but nothing official has been decided," she said.

"I'm no expert at dating, but I think that's it, whether you said so or not," I replied. Then, I told her about how April and Sam were dating in her reality and how it's been haunting me ever since.

"Isn't he your best friend? Well, one of them?" she asked.

"Yes! I've never seen him as anything but a friend until I spent a month in April's life. Now I can't unsee him in that role, or unfeel his kiss on my lips," I replied.

"And of course, you can't tell your friends about it because they'd think you were crazy," she said, nodding in understanding.

"And I've had the same feeling about your portrait of me as a writer. I thought I could leave it alone and just wait and see. But now I have another reason to have a peek," I said, getting excited again at the idea of having Gary for a stepdad. I asked her if she remembered him from some of the other's realities.

"I wish my mom would meet him! Maybe I should nudge her toward that dating app," she replied, pensive.

"It feels like cheating, but I have to know," I said. She laughed.

"It's not cheating, silly. That's why we come to Clarity Castle. To find clarity, answers, to choose what suits us best. How can we know what suits us if we don't try it out first? Nana always says, 'you can't make a cake…'" she started.

I finished the famous expression, "without cracking some eggs!" and we both laughed. This was so much fun. Like having a best friend and a sister all rolled into one.

"Ok, what would you like to see? Is there a date in particular?" she asked.

"I have no idea, but maybe pick a day where I'll see something relating to writing, Mom and Gary, and Sam and me," I said, aware I sounded like someone ordering from a catalogue.

She closed her eyes and seemed to be mentally flipping through the month. Then she smiled and opened her eyes. "I have the perfect day!" she said and took one of my hands before I knew what she was on about.

* * *

THERE WAS A LABOUR DAY PARTY AT OUR HOUSE! IT WAS THE FIRST WE'D ever hosted. The weather was fantastic and there were quite a few people in the pool. In addition to Mel, Julie, and Sam, there were some other kids of various ages I didn't recognize.

Mom and Gary were in a hot tub I guessed we're getting in the next five months. *Gary!* Nana was in there with them with what had to be her boyfriend because he was nibbling on her ear. Gross!

Even Uncle Riley was here, grilling burgers on the BBQ. I looked around to see Aunt Felicia, and there she was, serving margaritas fresh from the blender. I looked back at the kids in the pool, and realized they were Chase and Evan with their girlfriends. I hadn't seen them in so long.

Just then, Sam grabbed me by the waist, planted a kiss smack on my lips and launched us both into the pool. When we came up for air, he said, "we have to win this one!" He went back underwater, scooped up my legs and emerged with me on his shoulders. Chase and Even did the same, and Mel had Julie on her shoulders. It was some kind of volleyball game.

Within minutes, Chase and Mandy were crowned the ultimate champions and we were being called out of the pool to eat.

I went to my room to change out of my wet bathing suit. As I was about to leave my room, I saw an envelope on my desk. It hadn't been there this morning. Maybe Mom had forgotten to check the mailbox on Friday and Gary had stopped on the way back from getting some ice this morning.

It was from the local bank. It read, '*Dear Ms. Knox, we are happy to inform you that your essay titled "Change your thoughts, change your life" has been selected as one of the three finalists in our annual young writers' contest...*'

What? I hadn't entered any writing contest, nor had I written that essay. Oh, right. I hadn't done those things, yet. The letter went on to say that the finalists and their families were invited to an official reading after which the judges would announce the winning essay. The winner would receive a scholarship, in trust, for their post-secondary education, of three thousand dollars. Wow!

I rushed out holding the letter in one hand and my wet bathing suit in the other.

* * *

MY HANDS WERE STILL HOLDING THE INVISIBLE OBJECTS WHEN WE arrived back at the Castle. I guessed I had my answers. Yes, on all fronts. I still had mixed feelings about the Sam thing.

As though she was reading my mind, September said, "remember, you have free will. And so does Sam, your mom, and Gary. It can all happen exactly like that if things keep going the way they have. But anyone can change their minds and go in another direction. So, don't worry about it. It's just another one of a million possibilities," she said.

We chatted some more about her and Max. Then she helped me clarify my mixed feelings about Sam. In the end, the important thing was to let things happen naturally and see where they led. No pushing, but no resisting either. I thought it was great advice. I thanked her for taking the time and we both went back to our lives to get ready for bed.

CHAPTER TWENTY-NINE

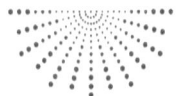

THAT NIGHT, I WAS INTENT ON FINDING OUT WHAT HAD HAPPENED TO April. Surely if she had disappeared for good, they would have replaced her, and we would have been called to witness the new April's memories. As it stood, I had no idea how to retrieve the updated month of March from April's reality.

When I got to the yellow room, April was there wearing her usual debate club outfit. So far so good. As I neared, she got up and hugged me. She was smiling, so I guess it worked out all right.

"How did it go?" I blurted out, too curious to wait for her to show me.

"It worked!" she said triumphantly. "Well, the main goal was achieved. As soon as I went back, I started hounding my dad every chance I had, providing as many details as I could remember. At first, he brushed me off. Then, after he'd told Mom I was acting weird, they had me see a shrink. That was the worst. They thought I was crazy, having delusions. Thankfully, the shrink was really good, and she convinced them that other than this bit about fraud, I was perfectly well adjusted and sane," she explained.

My hand was on my mouth, eyes wide with horror. That was the ultimate nightmare, having your parents think you're crazy. I took her hand in sympathy and sighed with relief when she said the shrink had been on her side.

"That's when he started quizzing me about the details. There was no way I could have known about the opportunity he would be presented with. It hadn't been in the papers, and he hadn't talked about it with Mom, so it wasn't the result of eavesdropping. Eventually, he told me to leave the matter to him and he would sort it out. I didn't have to worry about it anymore," she continued.

"I was still a little worried, especially when he and Mom announced our family trip to Cozumel. When I cornered him about it, he said he and Mom had been planning it since January because he'd gotten a huge bonus at the end of the year. I relaxed a little. Even more so when, in a whisper, he added that it was best if he was out of the country when the arrests were made," she said. I nodded.

From what I remembered, however, that had led to a rather stressful arrival at the Montreal airport and I told her so.

She grinned and held out her hand. I looked at her sideways, hesitating. I had not enjoyed my trip the last time. Tired of waiting, she grabbed my hand by herself.

* * *

I HAD FORGOTTEN HOW MUCH I ENJOYED THE TRIP TO MEXICO BEFORE the resulting ordeal. It was even better the second time around. Mom and Dad were even more relaxed, and it was an amazing week.

Upon our return, no agents assaulted us. We loaded up the car, stopped for dinner on the way home and made it back to Cowansville around eight. After unloading the car, Dad went back out to get groceries. Mom made us empty and put away our luggage and she had a load of laundry started before Dad came back. She hated having stuff lying around. Then she started whipping up a batch of muffins for the next morning. Though Penny and I had a ped day on Monday, it was back to work for Mom and Dad.

The rest of the month was dramatically different. While we were away, arrests had been made and the office had closed down for the week. Early Monday morning, Dad's boss called and asked him to come into the office to answer some routine questions so they could resume their operations. Dad told the truth, omitting my insider knowledge, and was cleared of any implications.

Instead of visiting Dad in jail every weekend, we had the standard busy family schedule. Mom and Dad had date night on Friday nights and Nana came over when she wasn't on a trip somewhere. On Saturdays, Penny had swimming lessons in the mornings, and we played family games at night. On Sundays, Mom and Dad often had brunch with friends before heading to the grocery store for the week's provisions.

April's life had greatly improved, but I still wouldn't trade places with her.

If it had been up to me, I would have spent more time with Penny. She was such a great little sister. Between the debate team, homework, and the time spent with Sam, I barely saw her during the week. I could always request follow-up visits.

I was a little torn about Dad, though. Since I hadn't grown up with him, I didn't miss having him around. Oddly enough, I regretted Gary's absence more than Dad's. Though I felt somewhat disloyal admitting it, even to myself, the truth was that Gary suited Mom better. In all the lives I had seen him in, she was happier, more relaxed. With Dad, she was harder, more driven in her career, and focused on material things. Gary made Mom fun!

Meanwhile, I got a good look at April and Sam's relationship. There were subtle differences that weren't due to the fact that Sam and I were only now starting to explore our feelings for each other.

Because April was so driven in school and had a clear path set out for her future, which coincided with Sam's plans, they were more of a power couple than anything else. It was as though they had decided they were stronger together and made a pact to help each other reach their individual and common goals. They'd set a very definite course for their lives, convinced they were in it for the long haul.

Who decides they're getting married at fifteen? They had it all mapped out: finish high school, get married, move to the city, attend law school, spend their summers interning at the best firms in Montreal, Toronto, and Vancouver, pass the bar, join elite firms, buy a house, have two kids.

It made my skin crawl just thinking about this ten-year plan. I'd only just found out I had a way with words and may or may not become a writer. Clearly, April was going to use those words to write briefs. But who was I to judge, in the end? She and Sam seemed content. I just wondered what that meant for my relationship with my Sam.

Would it be like Dad and Gary for Mom? Would dating me alter Sam's present? His future? For the better or worse?

My Sam was nowhere near as driven as he was in this reality. Or maybe I didn't know him intimately enough. I could see how Sam and I would make a great team; we were great friends and great study partners. But I was hoping the friendship would be the basis of any relationship we might develop. I wanted us to help each other grow, and, of course, I wanted Sam to reach his goals and would help in any way I could. But, to me, a romantic relationship was supposed to be, well, romantic.

Though I wasn't ready for raging hormones and the level of physical intimacy I saw in couples around me, I was hoping for more emotional intimacy. I was ready to have a best friend, without dropping Mel and Julie.

No, I didn't want April's life, but I was happy it had worked out for her. And I was happy I had visited both versions. It had been a golden opportunity to sort out what I didn't want, which was a step closer to figuring out what I did want.

CHAPTER THIRTY

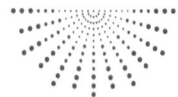

With the milder weather, it was no surprise that kids flocked outside at lunchtime. On our ride yesterday, the gang had decided to meet at our usual spot. However, when I got there the only one sitting at the table was Sam. I tried to remind myself that there was no reason for this to be awkward.

"Hey! Are the others running late?" I asked as I sat across from him. He frowned at the change in routine. I normally sat next to Sam, but if no one else came, it would look weird.

"Mel had a last-minute play rehearsal and Julie's mom picked her up a few minutes before the bell. Seems there was a cancellation at the orthodontist she's been trying to get in to see," he said. I checked my phone to see if Mel and Julie had messaged me, but there was nothing.

"How do you know all this? They didn't put it in the group text," I replied with a pout.

He laughed and started unpacking his lunch. "I saw Mel on my way here, and she told me about Julie because they were both in French class together before lunch," he explained.

I got my own lunch out and started eating. There hadn't been enough time or leftovers to put together an envy-invoking lunch. I had tossed a salad this morning and thrown in leftover pieces of salmon from the night before and grabbed a fruit cup for dessert.

Sam was staring at me. "Did you pack your own lunch?" he asked.

"Yes…" I replied, my right eyebrow shooting up in question.

"Is your mom out of town?" he asked, stuffing a piece of chicken salad sandwich he'd gotten out of the vending machine again.

"No, why? Did you want to have an out-of-control teenage party?" I scoffed.

He puffed out laughing. "No, silly. It's just I've never seen you with such a sad lunch," he replied.

"I'll have you know that it's a perfectly nutritious lunch. It has all the food groups, it's low carb, high protein, and high in omega threes," I replied in a huff.

He put his hands out in a pacifying gesture. "Of course it is. I'm sorry. I wasn't judging. I just meant it looked like your mom had abandoned you is all," he said with a pained expression.

I guess we weren't used to spending time alone without having homework as a buffer. He'd just given me an opening, and I latched onto it.

"That's because she's dating this new guy, Gary," I said, and we spent the next thirty minutes dissecting this new piece of information. Finally, a few minutes before the bell, as we were walking back towards the main doors, Sam casually asked if I wanted to come to see him swim at the competition in Sherbrooke on Saturday afternoon.

"I'll be leaving early in the morning on the bus with the team, but my family will drive in after lunch to watch the finals. I'm guaranteed a spot in the relay, and I might also be swimming in another event," he added.

"Yeah, sure. Are Mel and Julie coming?" I asked, innocently.

"With my brother in the car, there's only room for one extra person and my mom suggested I invite you," he said, looking straight ahead and acting like this was a regular occurrence.

He was clearly nervous about this and I honestly did want to see him swim in a race. I'd only ever seen him compete here in Cowansville. I tried to remember what September had said. I didn't need to overthink this.

"Yeah, sure. That sounds like a lot of fun. I just need to run it by my mom, but since I would be going with your parents, I'm sure she'll say yes. Thanks for asking!" I replied and clamped my mouth shut before I started to babble.

Thankfully, the bell rang, and he dashed off to get to the pool on time with a "later!" while I headed for my science class.

* * *

I WAS ON THE BUS WHEN I HEARD HER THE FIRST TIME. SINCE I HAD MY earbuds in, I took them out and looked around, thinking someone on the bus was talking to me. When the call came again, I put them back and tried my best to talk inside my head without looking like a moron.

I hadn't yet mastered this skill. I usually preferred to talk out loud like there was actually someone with me. But that wasn't an option right this minute. So, in my mind, I said, "I'm in the bus, can I get back to you in about five minutes?" She replied it wasn't a problem and before she tuned out, I asked who I was supposed to 'call' back. It was May. Pandemic Girl. Interesting.

When I got home, Mom was there. I gave her a hug, grabbed an apple, and told her I was going for a quick walk. I would head for the woods. Even if I talked out loud on my way there, people would think I was chatting over Bluetooth.

"Hey, May. What's up?" I asked.

"Hey, March. Do you have time for a chat?" she asked.

"I'm heading to the Castle site, physically I mean. I can meet you inside as soon as I can sit somewhere safe," I replied.

"I'm there now!" she exclaimed before adding, "you know that little path behind the gate, it goes up to a knoll. I'm sitting there. Hardly anyone comes by here. If they do, I just look like I'm meditating."

"Sounds perfect. I'll do that too," I said and picked up the pace. When I got there, I was looking down at where the Castle should be. I wish it was a real castle. The view of the lake here was a little obstructed by the trees, but similar to the view from one of the Castle's parapets. I found a log and sat down. Clearing my mind, I was instantly there.

She was sitting by the window looking out when I came in. I walked over to look out the window. I hadn't ever taken the time to see what the view was. It was facing east. From here, you could see a few outbuildings tucked in between the tall trees.

"There are horses in the stable," said May in a dreamy voice.

"Really? Can we go see them?" I asked excitedly.

"I can't see why not," she answered getting up from the window seat.

Neither of us knew if there were any outer doors on the eastern part of the Castle. We knew there was a door leading to the courtyard and we thought that if we couldn't find another, we'd go out through there.

There was a door, and only a few doors down from the yellow room. The configuration was identical to the western side of the Castle I had entered from the courtyard. The outer door must have been used by the serving staff because it was accessed by going down a half flight of stairs.

We made our way to the biggest of the buildings. It was shorter than the Castle, perhaps only two stories. It was about as wide as a street and had to be at least a half kilometer in length, but on the outside, it looked just like the Castle. I had seen buildings like this one in magazines. I think they started converting castle stables into apartments at some point.

These stables were filled with horses and the usual stable paraphernalia. And there were quite a few people working inside. No, not people, versions of me! It still boggled my mind that everyone at the Castle was a version of me.

"I wish I could live here," said May as we found our way to the stable boxes. Neither of us knew anything about horses so we stayed at a safe distance.

"Me too!" I replied earnestly. "I wonder if there are bedrooms, and if someone prepares food from the kitchens," I said.

"I think some of us do live here, though I'm not sure how that works. Do you think we have to die in our reality to move here permanently?" she asked.

"Maybe this is our version of Heaven," I said and we both nodded. The horses were pretty, but they were also smelly. Without discussing it, we headed back out and followed a worn patch of grass that led to a large paddock where more horses could be seen grazing and hanging out.

We rested our arms on the fence and stared out at them. I figured May would tell me what was on her mind when she was ready. I was in no hurry. This place was amazing and, since time didn't pass here the way it did at home, I had nowhere better to be just now.

"So, it's mid-June for me, like it's mid-April for you," she started. I nodded but said nothing. "This is going to sound so stupid, but I think I want to merge realities with you," she said and waited for me to respond.

My heart gave a little flutter. My gut reaction was a negative one. I didn't want to share my life, my body, with her. That would be weird, intrusive. Then I remembered that she was me. That her reality was almost identical to mine in all aspects except the pandemic raging in hers. Of course, she wanted out. She had probably waited for April's crisis to be over before bringing it up.

"It's not stupid. What's stupid is that I was wondering if your life was better than mine after I spent some time there," I said with a laugh. Her shocked expression was priceless. "I got over it real quick when I realized I could manifest the good parts of your life into mine without having to endure the hardships," I quickly added.

"Don't get me wrong, I love my life. But there have been a few developments that are now tipping the scales and making me want to make a move," she said.

Then it dawned on me. This was about Sam! She was two months ahead of me. She had likely gone to the swimming competition. But no, there weren't any competitions in her reality. The swim team was hoping to resume their activities with the April safety measures, but there hadn't been any guarantees. Maybe it wasn't about Sam.

"Is this about Mom?" I asked, worried.

"Not entirely. She started seeing Gary a few months ago. It's been a bit of a challenge since they have to stay two meters apart, but I think they've grown close in other ways. Taking their time to get to know one another," she said.

"Yeah, Mom's going on her third date with him in my reality. I'm very excited," I replied. She nodded in agreement.

"I've had a similar experience with Sam…" she said trailing off. I smiled and nudged her with my shoulder.

"Go on," I urged her.

"The swim team still hasn't been allowed to resume their activities, so Sam has a lot of free time. He's got a training program to do which includes running and bodyweight resistance training, but it only lasts about an hour per day. Since he lives closest to our house, he and I have been spending more time together, taking walks, going for bike rides, that kind of thing," she explained.

"And now you're kinda dating but you can't take it to the next level?" I asked, seeing where this is going. She blushed and kicked some pebbles with her shoes, staring down at them with great interest.

Finally, she said, "it's not what your thinking!"

I laughed and nudged her again. "You forget we are basically the same person. There is no way I'd be ready for anything other than holding hands, hugs, and maybe a first kiss down the line," I said, teasing her. "I get it," I added. She blew out a relieved breath and sagged against me. I put my arm around her and rested my head on hers, aware I was giving a new name to self-soothing.

CHAPTER THIRTY-ONE

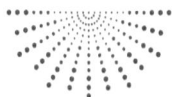

That night, while May was doing the required rounds of memory visits, I had requested a meeting with the Teacher.

"What will it feel like?" I asked about the possible merge.

"It won't feel like anything. Once the ceremony is completed, May's consciousness will merge with yours and when you wake up the next day, you will feel like yourself. Henceforth, you might make slightly different choices because you'll have an added perspective, but you won't be aware of it as being different from your own," she explained.

"But what happens to May's reality?" I asked.

"Her reality will continue as it was. She will continue to be part of the group as May," replied the Teacher, sipping the tea I had refused.

"But won't that be weird?" I asked.

"For whom?" asked the Teacher, her head cocked to one side.

Good question. "For me, for May, for everyone, really," I tried.

"Oh, yes. I see. I'm sorry, I thought you understood that once the merge is completed, none of you will remember how things were before," she said.

Ah, an important detail.

"Okay, so if and when we do this, May's consciousness will merge with mine while we are asleep. When I wake up, I won't see a differ-ence and I won't remember the merge. When she wakes up, she'll be in my life as me, and won't remember her old reality. Did I get that right?" I asked rubbing the muscles above my eyebrows.

"Yes," she exclaimed.

"So there really isn't a downside to this at all," I said.

"None at all. And as you get used to the process, and maintain a high vibration, you see it will become a regular, and speedier, occur-rence. Instead of painstakingly working on individual manifestations in your own reality, you'll find that many of your desires are already grouped together in another reality. It's far simpler to jump into a new reality, don't you think?" she asked. I nodded. It still felt like a shortcut to me, but that's why I was here. To realize life wasn't supposed to be so hard and that, with a little help, I could literally have, be, or do whatever I wanted.

At the same time, both our heads shot up. We were being called to the ceremony room. Already? She was right, it was a much faster process once everyone in the group had access to their memories.

The teacher and I materialized in the room where the others were assembled in their respective spots. I went to stand under my portrait, scrutinizing it in case September had added any new clues as to my life down the road. It hadn't changed and I winked at her before facing forward.

May went to the circle and spoke her intention. No one objected, and it was done. As simple as that. I wanted to stay and talk to the Guide, but as soon as May returned to her portrait, I blacked out.

CHAPTER THIRTY-TWO

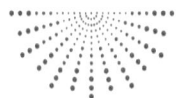

THE REST OF THE WEEK WAS UNEVENTFUL. MOM HAD NOT ONLY AGREED to my going to the swimming competition with Sam's parents, but she was also overjoyed I'd have somewhere to be while she was out with Gary.

Gary picked her up on Saturday morning around nine. Since the cat was out of the bag, she introduced him briefly when he came to the door, then gave me a quick hug and told me to have a good time.

"You too!" I said, waving them off from the porch. I was itching to hug Gary, but that would have been weird. I'd just need to bide my time.

I spent the morning studying for my upcoming math and science tests. I wondered if the teachers planned on giving us tests and assignments all in the same week. We'd started a new novel in English and another in French. Both had chapter questions that had to be handed in on Monday.

I went out on the deck to eat my lunch and read some pages from the French book. It wasn't bad. It was the first novel of a trilogy about ants. *Right?* After a few chapters, I wondered if this could have been the inspiration for that animated movie called *Antz*. After a little

149

digging on the internet, I found that it wasn't, but I still decided I would watch the movie soon.

After lunch, I got my things together and waited for Sam's parents. His mom had called and said they'd pick me up around one in the evening. At the last minute, I grabbed my French novel and added it to my bag. If there was time to kill, I'd be happy to have it along.

Sam's relay race was scheduled for three in the evening. We got there with about fifteen minutes to spare and had time to find a good spot to watch from. This was a regional competition and there were a lot of spectators. The noise level was very high, and I debated putting my earbuds in just to drown out the chaos. But Sam's mom kept telling me stuff about the other swimmers and the other teams and it would have been rude.

Finally, they called the teams for the four-hundred-meter relay race. Sam was doing one hundred meters of butterfly. It was a tight race and they came in second. The team and the coach seemed pleased.

We checked the board and saw they would be doing two of the final races up next. Sam had all of fifteen minutes to catch his breath before he was called for the fifty-meter freestyle race. He totally nailed it and won the race. I was hooting and jumping with his family, waving like a maniac so he knew where we were, on the off chance he couldn't hear us.

With a huge grin, he waved back at us and pointed to the spot where they were giving out medals and trophies for the day. I took about as many pictures as his mom did with my phone. I was so proud of him I could have burst.

We waited for him out in the lobby. After about thirty minutes, Sam appeared, two medals around his neck. The gold medal for the freestyle race and a bronze one for the relay. We dutifully applauded our fearless winner.

His parents took us out to a celebratory dinner in Sherbrooke. Sam wanted carbs so we went to that Italian chain that had a bread bar. I hadn't been in years and was happy to see they still had the tarragon butter I loved so much. I had to be careful to leave room for the lasagna I had ordered. In the end, I didn't have to worry because Sam finished everyone's plates.

Though I'd had dinner at Sam's plenty of times over the years, I'd never gone out with them. It could have been awkward, but it wasn't. No one in his family made any off-putting comments about this being a date or anything and his brother was really sweet. I felt like I was part of the family and it helped me embrace the possibility of Sam and me as a couple.

After dessert, we headed back home. It was past nine when we got home and, again, there was no awkwardness. I thanked Sam's parents, waved to Curtis, gave Sam the usual hug, and told him I'd message him the next day.

Mom was home when I came into the house. I had texted her before we left the restaurant so she wouldn't worry, but she said she'd only gotten home a moment ago herself. She was wearing her robe and about to jump in the shower. I told her to go ahead and we could have our chat when she was done.

While I waited, I looked at the pictures I'd taken of Sam's races. I chose my favourites and sent them to him. He thanked me for the pictures and for coming to the race. I told him I'd had a great time and to thank his parents again for me. My phone rang just then. It was Sam.

"Hey, what's up?" I asked.

"I just wanted to tell you how much it meant to me that you were there today," he said.

"You already did, goofball," I replied, laughing, but I stopped when I noticed he wasn't laughing. There was a beat, then two. I waited.

"So, do you want to come to my house tomorrow, to study for the math test?" he asked tentatively.

We studied quite efficiently via videoconference, but I didn't point that out. Instead, I countered with, "how about you come here? My mom will think it's too much of an imposition to spend two days in a row with your family."

"Yeah, sure. What time?" he asked. I wanted to check with Mom so I told him I would text him the time before I went to bed.

"Goodnight, Clare," he said into the phone.

"Goodnight, Sam," I replied. It was the first weird thing we'd said to each other so far. Up until now, we'd been regular friends. We wouldn't have called each other, nor would we have said goodnight. I felt a little giddy.

Mom was in the kitchen making tea when I wrapped up with Sam. She asked about the race and I told her about dinner and my plans to study with Sam the next day. I could tell she was dying to comment on the change in our relationship. But the extent of the grin I was still sporting must have made her change her mind.

"Tell him to come over around two, that way he can stay for dinner," she said.

"Thanks for not being weird about this, Mom," I said and gave her a quick hug. I deftly maneuvered the conversation back to her, before she could tease me. "So how was your date with Gary? It can't have been a very romantic date if you had dinner in your hiking clothes, all sweaty and dirty," I said with a smile.

"I think *that* date comes next," she said, tongue in cheek. "The hike was fantastic. We have a similar pace and we both stopped way too often to take pictures. We had dinner at a pub on the way home. A lot of people stop there for a beer and a bite after being outdoors, we fit right in," she replied.

"So, it went well if you're considering the next date," I said, sitting on the edge of my seat looking way too eager. She didn't seem to notice, or perhaps she didn't care.

"Yes, it went well. I like him. He's easy to talk to and communicates clearly. I never have to guess what he means. He's the kind of person everyone gets along with," she said a little wistfully. If I was hoping to get more out of her, it wasn't going to be tonight.

She checked her watch, got up and told me it was time to hit the sack.

CHAPTER THIRTY-THREE

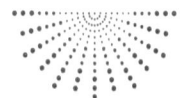

Sam and I started spending more and more time together but hadn't yet come out to the rest of our friends that we were becoming more than friends. We were enjoying life in our little bubble. There was so much I hadn't known about Sam. Like the fact that he used to go fishing after school with his granddad and was so sad when he died that his parents had registered him in the after-school swim team program to keep him busy.

And I had somehow missed a million little nuances about his appearance. I always knew Sam was handsome, but I had taken his sandy hair, olive complexion, and brown eyes for granted. The more I looked at him, the more I saw. For one thing, his natural hair colour was chestnut, but the constant contact with chlorine had washed it out.

"I'd love to grow my hair to my shoulders," he had said once, taking me completely by surprise. He explained that he kept it short so it was easier to put on the swim cap. Because he cut it so regularly, it was never coarse or dry the way other swimmers' hair was. I loved to run my hand through it, feeling the shape of his skull, the heat from his head. I sometimes just let my hand rest on the top and said I was absorbing his genius.

In response, Sam would coil my long blonde tresses around his arm and slowly pull it out to admire the whirlpool he'd created before my hair went back to its perfectly straight curtain against my back.

"You're like a mermaid, sitting on a rock, calling me to swim out to sea," he said, gazing at me in wonder. His eyes weren't merely brown. They were flecked with gold and took on a greenish sheen when he stared at me like that. It was like he was leaving golden sprinkles wherever his gaze fell.

"I can't be a mermaid, I'm not a good enough swimmer. But I do have magical abilities," I replied and told Sam about my trips to the Castle, but I could tell Sam didn't entirely believe me. I mean, he believed I was dreaming about it at night, but not the part about visiting during the daytime or about the others communicating through telepathy. He thought I must have been napping those other times. Like when I was relaxing in yoga class.

Either way, the important thing was that he didn't think I was crazy and thought it was cool as it was helping me do better in school and not worry so much. It felt good talking and opening up to each other, discussing our innermost secrets and desires.

In May, Mel started daily rehearsals at lunch and after school for the upcoming play. Julie started dating James, a guy from the robotics program. They were immediately inseparable and insufferable.

Meanwhile, I was crushing my school work and exams and, because Sam and I weren't playing kissy-face all the time, a lot of our time together was spent studying. We hadn't yet gotten around to the first kiss, anyway. With finals coming up, and our hesitance about how we didn't want to ruin our friendship, we were taking it slow. With my birthday coming up in June, we decided to come out to our friends before I had my party.

As a treat for nailing the regional math exam, Sam and I went to the movies on a Tuesday afternoon during the first exam week. Neither of us had an exam the following day and could afford to blow off some steam.

After the movie, we were walking hand in hand down Main street when we crossed paths with Mel and her mom. Mel was an excellent actress but the initial look of shock, then anger, she wore was real. Her gaze was fixed to our clasped hands and the heat of it felt like she was boring a hole in them with a laser. Instinctively, I let go of Sam's hand, but he only grasped it more firmly.

"Hi, Mrs. Darby. Hi, Mel," he said smoothly, plastering a smile on his beautiful face. He squeezed my hand and I did the same.

Mel's face was immediately transformed into a vision of joy and benevolence. She rushed toward us and gave us a joint hug, kissing each of our cheeks.

"Look at you! I didn't know you were dating!" she exclaimed as though this was the best news ever. Like I said, she was a great actress.

Her mom was uncomfortable and said, "it's good to see you Sam and Clare. I hope all is well with your parents?" she asked, smiling as genuinely as she could.

We both nodded and replied with the usual platitudes.

"Good, good. We really must be on our way, Mel has an appointment at the orthodontist," she said and started pulling Mel away down the street.

She turned and waved at us. "See you at school!" she said in a chipper voice, but her eyes were slicing us apart.

On the way home, I was a nervous wreck. "She's going to tell Julie and then we'll be in trouble. We shouldn't have waited so long to tell them. I'm such an idiot," I said, barely taking a breath between each sentence.

Sam let go of my hand and put an arm around me. "Relax, they'll get over it. We've been friends forever, this won't change anything," he said. I leaned into him but couldn't shake the feeling of impending doom. He was being naive. This would change everything.

When we got to my house, he hugged me tight and told me not to overthink this.

"And don't try to do damage control, either," he said, waving a finger in warning. "Let it unfold. Let Mel tell Julie and get her feelings out. Let her deal with Julie's reaction. That way we can deal with both of them, together, once the bulk of their rant has passed," he added as he started walking away. He blew me a kiss and made a call me later gesture. I caught the kiss and held it to my chest as I watched him walk down the street.

I went inside and responded to the automatic truancy message the school sent when we didn't show up for the afternoon study periods. Mom was fine with my studying at home and it would save her the hassle of having to leave a message on the school's answering service.

With that chore out of the way, I got dinner started as I stewed about the situation. Once the salad was done and the stuffed pork loin Mom had prepared was in the oven, I tried to focus on my science notes. I was itching to do exactly what Sam had advised against. With the oven running, I couldn't go for a walk. I needed to fix this. I needed to do something.

Then I thought of calling one of the girls. Which one? April seemed like the best option as she might have dealt with a similar situation, though she didn't have the same friends. January was the most optimistic and December was the most Zen. I went with April, but I couldn't reach her. I tried the other two and got no response. I sighed in frustration.

I went to lie on my bed, cleared my mind as best I could, and tried to go to the Castle. Why wasn't it working? At the sound of the oven timer, I gave up and went to turn it off. It was getting on my nerves. Taking the pork out of the oven, the smoke alarm started screeching and all I could do was yell at it to shut up. That's when Mom came in.

"Are you okay honey?" she asked as I started to cry. She rushed over, torn between embracing me and shutting up the bellowing reminder she needed to clean the oven.

She chose wisely, waving the cardboard in the air while I cracked the window open.

"What happened?" she said, stroking my back soothingly. "Did you have a fight with Sam?"

Through sniffles and sobs, I told her what had happened. She grabbed a tissue from the box near her desk and gave it to me. She brushed the hair out of my face so it wouldn't get caught in my snot.

"Oh honey, you're making way too much of this," she said trying her best not to smile. "For a minute there, I thought you'd failed your math exam." She went to the fridge to pour herself a glass of rosé wine. She shrugged out of her suit jacket and asked if I wanted to eat inside or out. I preferred to eat inside as the warmth of June had attracted the usual stinging critters.

We set the table and started to eat. Though we had perfectly healthy muffins for dessert, Mom asked if I wanted to walk to the ice cream shop after dinner. This was a sure-fire way of instantly improving my mood.

On the way, I told her what Sam had said and she agreed with his sage advice.

"Do you have any reason to believe either Julie or Mel have secret feelings for you or Sam?" she asked while we waited on our order. Mom had chosen amaretto-flavoured frozen yogurt while I had asked for a chocolate-vanilla twist dipped in chocolate and nuts.

I thought about her question. Julie was still dating James and from the looks of their steamy make-out sessions by her locker, I'd say it was safe to say Julie didn't have any designs on either of us. As for Mel, she seemed really angry. There was nothing in her behaviour towards me that would lead me to believe she'd had a crush on me. And I'd never noticed any towards Sam either, though it was possible she behaved differently when she was alone with him.

"I don't think so," I replied, not one hundred percent sure.

"Well, then it's a breach of trust. No one likes to be the last to know something. The fact that you were parading about town probably made her feel like you were ready for everyone to know but her," said Mom, retrieving our treat.

Since we had things to do, we decided to eat on the way home.

"We weren't parading in town, Mom!" I exclaimed indignantly. "We were just holding hands!"

"I know, I know. But you get what I'm saying," she replied. I nodded and we walked in silence as we savoured our treats. I sighed in contentment and gave Mom a shoulder bump.

"Thanks, Mom," I said.

She kissed my temple and replied, "anytime, baby girl."

CHAPTER THIRTY-FOUR

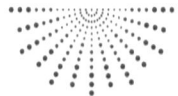

THAT NIGHT I FINALLY MADE IT TO THE CASTLE. THE YELLOW ROOM WAS empty so I headed for the elevator that would take me down to the Teacher's office. I could try calling her, but I was still full of nervous energy. I had followed Mom and Sam's advice and resisted the urge to contact Mel and Julie. In fact, I had used the landline to call Sam before bed and didn't use my phone or tablet at all to ensure my own compliance.

On the way, I crossed paths with a Guide. There was no way of knowing if she was the same guide who had presided over our last two ceremonies. She was wearing the same long, pale pink robe tied with a magenta sash. And, of course, she looked like an older version of me. I put her at a little over fifty. She had the same number of grey hairs Mom had, but that couldn't be a very accurate measure of someone's age.

"Hello, do you have a moment?" I asked her. She stopped, smiled, and said she had all the time in the world. I smiled in response. Indeed.

"I was going to find my Teacher, but perhaps you could help me. I need guidance. Should I make a formal request? Is there a procedure I need to follow?" I asked with as much reverence as I could muster.

"I am here, now, so that makes me your Guide," she replied. She asked if I wanted to walk with her and I nodded. She led the way to one of the courtyard doors. The children were playing outside, and it was a treat to see all the mini-mes laughing and running about.

"When can I meet with the little ones?" I asked suddenly. She smiled fondly at the little ones playing in the sandbox. They were so adorable with their chubby hands and feet, wiggling their toes in the sand.

"When you are no longer part of a group, you will be able to access your younger and older selves," she replied, pushing the coach doors leading to the outer grounds.

As we walked towards the lake, I told her about being unable to reach the members of my group or the Castle that afternoon. She nodded in understanding.

"Do you remember how you got here the first time?" she asked. I did.

"I was blissed out, basking in the sun," I said.

"Exactly. Your vibration was high, and the Castle appeared," she said. This was true. "How did you feel yesterday afternoon?" she asked.

"Worried about my friends hating me, then frustrated when I couldn't reach anyone for help, then irritated about everything," I answered.

"Did you notice how it got from bad to worse?" she asked, and I nodded. "Did you ever get a chance to look up the emotional scale on the internet?" she inquired.

I blushed and shook my head. It had completely fled my mind. Things were going so well and then I'd started seeing Sam.

"Don't worry about it, but make sure you look into it sooner rather than later," she suggested.

"I promise!" I replied.

We had arrived at my favourite bench and she suggested we sit and watch the ducks.

"Those were negative emotions. Anything below contentment will keep you from your Knowing and therefore from the Castle. That's why it's imperative that you take daily steps to maintain or raise your vibration," she explained.

"Like what?" I asked.

"Like taking a walk, doing meditation, going out for an ice cream with your Mom," she replied with a wink.

I had taken notice of such practices in the others' realities but hadn't actually taken steps to integrate them into my life.

"Things were going so well, I guess I took it for granted that I could come here anytime I wanted from now on," I replied, hanging my head a little.

"It's important that you understand that you didn't do anything wrong. You weren't being punished. If anything, you were punishing yourself." She paused for a moment and smiled again. "Any emotion that is not based on love has to be based on fear. Do you know that feeling you get when you're gripped in fear? Your throat feels constricted, your gut twists, your whole body tightens."

"Yes! It's like some giant is wringing out the joy from your whole body," I replied.

"Exactly. Except you are the giant, twisting the hose through which life force, or love, is flowing. It's impossible to think clearly when you are cut off from the flow of love," she explained.

It made perfect sense.

"But how do I avoid getting scared, or angry, or frustrated? It might take years for me to master my thoughts and emotions like those Buddhist monks!" I wailed.

"You don't have to master your emotions, or even monitor your thoughts. You need to get out ahead of it. You always attract people and situations that match your vibration. By starting your day with a high vibration, you'll ensure you have a great day, every day!" said the Guide cheerfully.

"But I can't be happy all the time, can I?" I asked.

"No, and you don't have to. You just need to feel satisfied or content. Count your blessings, focus only on the things that are going well, and let the other things sort themselves out. When you have a bigger challenge, sort it out here, with us. Try out some solutions here before you try them out in your waking life," she suggested. At my confused expression, she added, "we'll teach you how to do that in time. But for now, when life throws you a curve, just go with it. It's just a game and you're here to win," she said.

She got up then and started walking back to the Castle. When I went to thank her, I saw she had disappeared into the wind.

I sat for a while longer, enjoying the sun on my face in the middle of the night.

CHAPTER THIRTY-FIVE

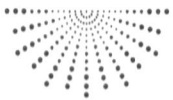

THE NEXT MORNING, I TOOK A PAGE FROM THE SPORTY VERSIONS OF ME and headed outside. There was no way I could jog, but I could walk my favourite trail to the lake. Mom, already seated outside with her coffee, had raised a quizzical eyebrow at my shorts and sneakers at such an early hour.

"I'm going for an early morning stroll," I said and left her to her meditative coffee sipping.

It was already warm, and I quickly shrugged out of my hoodie. I was happy I'd brought along my water bottle because I was parched in minutes. I was walking briskly as much for the exercise as for keeping this walk as short as possible. There would be no lollygagging today. I didn't have to waste the day away to raise my vibration.

Just feeling the sun on my face, hearing the birds chatting it up in the trees, and smelling the pines in the woods was enough to put me in a good mood. I walked the trail that followed the lake but didn't sit down. I'd been here last night! Besides, all the ducks were sunning themselves over on the dock before the boat attendant arrived for the day. I gave them a quick wave and was sure they all quacked in response.

When I got home, I was surprised to see a bike in our driveway.

Once inside, I saw who the owner was. It was Mel. She was eating a muffin at the kitchen counter chatting with Mom about the school play. The show was this Friday and she was very excited about it.

When she spotted me, she stopped talking and got up.

"Hi, Clare," she said. She looked nervous and I didn't know why. Maybe she'd tried to message me and, getting no response, decided to come here instead. I hadn't checked my phone when I woke up.

"Hi, Mel," I answered calmly, giving her space to say what she'd come to say.

"Do you want to ride to school on our bikes?" she suggested with a tentative smile. Relieved, I smiled too.

"Yeah, sure. In that case, I won't take a shower if we're going to get all sweaty on the way. I'll just change into school-approved attire," I said and went to my room. I hadn't planned on going to school this morning since I didn't have an exam, but I was going to take this olive branch. I could always pop in on the science remediation session and come back home. I stashed my stuff in my backpack, grabbed a muffin, and kissed Mom goodbye.

I ate the muffin on my way to retrieve my bike from the garage and we were off.

"So, I don't know if you read any of my messages from last night," she started, eyes focused on the road ahead.

"To be honest, I didn't. Sam and Mom suggested I just give you space," I replied.

"That's great. Be a friend and delete them all. I overreacted. I guess I just felt left out. Not that you and Sam were excluding me, but with Julie dating James, and you guys being a couple, I literally felt like the fifth wheel," she said.

"I'm so sorry we didn't tell you before. I guess we didn't want to rock the group dynamic until we knew that things would work out," I said.

"I get it. And, for the record, I would have done the same. It would just have been awkward for everyone if you'd said so right away and then found out it was a mistake," she replied.

"I'm so glad you came over this morning and we had this talk. How does Julie feel about it?" I asked her.

"She said she knew you guys would end up together and she was happy for you. I think she's so caught up in her own little love bubble that she wants everyone to be dating someone," she replied with a chuckle.

"So, still friends?" I asked sheepishly, giving her a sidelong glance.

"Always," she said, extending her fist for a bump. My hand went out to meet hers, but we nearly ended up colliding. We laughed so hard, we had to stop and catch our breath a block away from the school.

We were early so Mel asked for details about my budding relationship with Sam. I gave her the short version. There actually wasn't a long version anyway, we were still working on it. When I was done, we got back on our bikes and headed for the bike parking. I walked with her to her locker, wished her luck on her exam, and came back to get my bike.

I didn't need the remediation sessions and would be much more comfortable at home studying under the gazebo. On impulse, I headed for Sam's house. By then, it was past nine and he was home alone. We'd never been alone before, there was always someone around.

He invited me in and asked if I wanted anything to eat or drink. I declined. We sat on his couch, me still clutching my backpack I'd removed. We didn't say anything for at least thirty seconds. My heart was racing, and the beat was getting deafening in my ears.

I jumped when Sam took my backpack and put it on the floor. My hands started fidgeting so he took one of them. The other flitting on my lap like a fish out of water. He took that one too and pulled it so that I turned slightly to face him.

His eyes were on our hands, his thumb tracing an invisible pattern on my hand. He got up and pulled me up with him, pulling me a little closer still. He looked up then and I got the full force of his gaze.

Our eyes were locked, golden sparkles going back and forth. He smiled a slow smile. My lips curved into a matching expression. We stood there, holding hands, absorbed in the galaxy we had created between us. Our faces gravitating nearer and nearer until our lips met. Softly at first as though they had accidentally bumped into each other like asteroids. Then more firmly.

I smiled. He smiled. Our teeth clanked and we burst out laughing which only made our foreheads knock together. But instead of pulling away and rubbing at the bruise that was sure to form, we stayed there, foreheads touching like elephants in love.

"I love you, Clare Knox," he said in a clear, sure voice.

"I love you, Samuel Goodman," I replied in a breathy wonder.

We kissed again, serious now but in no hurry to answer the call of hormones that were starting to rage. Sam let go of my hands and wrapped his arms around me. This was the closest, tightest hug we'd ever exchanged. It felt amazing. It felt like love, friendship, security, excitement, and even a little bit of adventure all rolled into one. This was a high vibration. This was the highest vibration. It was pure bliss. The best day ever.

And I knew then and there, that if I wanted to feel that way every day, all I had to do was start the day with a walk like today, or a meditation like Mom did, or anything that would put me in a good mood. It was barely ten o'clock and I had already had an amazing day.

We finally pulled apart and Sam asked if Mom was at my house. When I said she was, he suggested we go to my house to study as his parents wouldn't like us being home alone and admitted he was having a hard time keeping his hands off me. I felt the same. We didn't need to jump each others' bones just because we were alone for the first time.

We had all the time in the world.

The End

If you enjoyed this book, would you consider leaving a review on Amazon, Bookbub, or Goodreads? Reviews help me reach new readers and improve my craft.

Read The Ancestors' Key, the first book in *The Evers Series*.

www.ingramcontent.com/pod-product-compliance
Lightning Source LLC
Chambersburg PA
CBHW020336260626
47156CB00004B/1553